THE SHATTERED AURORA

THE GRIMM STAR SAGA: FIRST LIGHT BOOK 3

J. DARLENE EVERLY

J. DARLENE EVERLY

THE SHATTERED AURORA

The Grimm Star Saga: First Light Book 3

Copyright © 2021 J. Darlene Everly

Hardcover: ISBN 978-1-954719-17-0
Paperback: ISBN 978-1-954719-16-3
Ebook: ISBN 978-1-954719-15-6
Library of Congress number:
First paperback edition May 2021.
Edited by Beth Hale, Magnolia Editing.
Cover art by Jupiter Alley.
Layout by Wishing Well Books.

❀ Created with Vellum

The Shattered Aurora is the final book in The Grimm Star Saga:
First Light,
but more stories from the world of The Grimm Star are coming
soon.
Keep an eye out for Song Of The Piper,
scheduled for publication in January of 2022.
It starts The Grimm Star Saga and may include some familiar
faces.
If you would like to be the first to hear about the next book in
this story world,
and get a free book in The Grimm Star Universe while you see
the others the author has written
and the other series coming out this year,
please go to jdarleneeverly.com and sign up for her newsletter.
Happily ever reading!

DEDICATION

This book is dedicated to my babies.

1

BRIAR

HE STARED OUT THE WINDOW IN THE GATHERING ROOM AGAIN AS the ship spun in orbit around their planet.

It was a struggle to remember to think of it as his planet, although it actually belonged more to him than some of the people who had already stepped foot on it. The underserving. The rejected. By rights, it belonged to people like him.

"Briar," Grandpa Kason said from behind him, and he curled his shoulders in response, not wanting to hear it. "We talked about this. You're going to have to stop and process before something happens again. I can't keep you in here if you keep pushing your luck."

"They shouldn't even be there," Briar said, ignoring Grandpa Kason, although he was sure it would mean less in his nightly delivery of food.

Grandpa Kason sighed and moved around to where Briar could see him. His mouth was turned down in a frown that aged him even more than he already was and managed to make Briar want to punch him at the same time.

"You know, it's only my influence giving you this chance."

Grandpa Kason's voice was hard and he narrowed his eyes as he leaned closer to Briar. "It would be a shame if you squandered it. There is still a lot of work for you to do to save our new home from the wrong sort."

He looked past the old man to watch as the ship turned the planet out of view again and nodded.

Being left alone was something he was still getting used to, but when the door shut behind the only person who visited him other than a medic who he had to pretend to be contrite and mildly untethered for, Briar was relieved.

Tucked under the edge of the weird cubby in the tiny closet near where he set his blanket and his pillow, Briar retrieved his hidden holo.

Keep moving forward mattered, but he kept being drawn back to the same file. He tapped at it until the recorded feeds from the spindles came up.

No matter how many times he watched as the citizens of the Wheel stepped foot on the planet for the first time, it sped up his heart rate and froze him in place.

It was beautiful and strange.

And he still couldn't decide if he truly did belong there, or if he thought the planet itself should have never existed.

2

———

TROYLUS

HE DROVE THE END OF THE SHOVEL INTO THE DIRT AND LEANED on the handle while he tilted his head back and spotted their sun.

Close enough to the right time, he decided. Five extra minutes of rest might give him the energy to use his ability even more than he usually did after he was done with a break and some lunch.

He stopped by the door to the interior of the spindle and keyed in the message to the panel just inside the alcove the door was in.

While the metal buttons in the narrow shadow created by the alcove were cool to the touch, he could barely see through the sweat dripping into his eyes.

All he could do as he turned away was hope he entered it all in correctly or he was going to get some weird ass food.

The brown grass under his boots crunched as he walked across it, wiping the sweat off his brow with the back of his hand.

It was still weird to have no hair tickling his skin on his face and his neck, but it was too gross when it stuck to him.

He made his way toward the shade cast by the spindle, its point buried in the ground, it still stretched into the sky. They were working on the other side of the spindle first, something about the winds and the way the biggest buildings in the burgh were supposed to be set up. He didn't pay much attention to the things the terraformers said about why they were building where they were first, other than to decide it was stupid.

"You know, she may not like the haircut," Obie said from his spot laying in the rough grass in the shade.

Passing into the dark space, it took a second for his eyes to adjust to the different light and he spotted Obie, a fellow star-walker with deep brown skin and dark brown hair from a different shift who he had told about his intention to get their work done as fast as possible and head to Zellendine.

Obie said he was untethered to do that for a girl.

But Troylus had laughed at him. He knew the only untethered thing about it was that he would have agreed with Obie before he and Zellendine happened.

He plopped down beside Obie, the grass as he landed on it sent up a cloud of bits floating into the air making him wave his hand around to try and stop it from sticking to his face as Obie coughed.

"Sorry," Troylus said, laughing as he laid back too.

"No, you're not."

He really wasn't, but he didn't answer; he just smiled and looked up at the pink and red sky.

"It's still funky," Troylus said, tossing a halfhearted gesture upward. "Any word?"

"Yeah, the storm is supposed to pass through the mountain range tomorrow, and then we'll have to see if the comms work again, but even if we have to hike all the way up there again, at least the sky won't look as pissed off." Obie rubbed his hands over his face and fell silent.

Obie was good friends with one of the terraforming crew and kept trying to get Troylus to hang out with them, but he didn't want to take the time.

"What I want to know is, are the temps always like this? And are they the same everywhere?" Obie grabbed the front of his uniform and flapped it so a bubble of air traveled up and down the length of him.

It was a good idea so Troylus copied him and sighed as the air let a cooler wash traverse his skin.

"Not to mention, what can we grow in this? And what animals will survive in this? My sister is assigned to the orchard, none of the conditions in there say that this would work for those plants or animals."

Obie nodded and tilted his head toward the mountains that flanked what would be the new burgh they were building.

"I didn't see much in the way of animals when we were up there, or even much for plants. Just a shit load of grass."

"Well, that's not great, is it?"

"Nope. Maybe this will be a short lived colonization and we will all have to move on before you even get to miss your girl very much."

Troylus shook his head and smiled. Too late, he missed her more than he could explain before they even took off.

"Yeah, I really want to see those reports from all the spindles. It should tell us a lot."

"It will tell you a lot maybe, but the rest of us will just be as happy to wait for the terraforming if it comes to that," Obie said, sounding borderline annoyed.

He probably was annoying to be around, he had a singular focus and was polite, but he didn't go out of his way to make friends.

"Good universe, this sucks," one of the other starwalkers said as he came into the shade with a whole group.

Watching them laugh and joke made Troylus even less likely to reach out and try to learn how to make friends with people other than the ones of his shift. The closest he had come was Imogene, and that was more bonding over their shared ability. Then he had left her behind, mostly even shoved her to a corner of his mind since their conversation.

Maybe that was for the best, and keeping himself focused and away from the others on this mission was probably for the best too.

Especially since they might hate him after they found out about the computers, if they knew he was one of the ones who put the information out there.

And, if he had his way, not only would not a damn one of them ever know that about him, but it would hopefully topple all the power structures of leadership and that would inevitably be a big mess.

No thanks, he thought. *No one needs to know shit.* A spot in some climate area that the terraformers said were good for plants and animals was the best option.

He, and Zellendine, and any of the people they told about their plan to get away who might think of it and want to join them after the breakdown needed to find the best climate to give them a real chance.

But that would only work if no one knew about their whole plan. And the best way to keep that true was to not get too friendly.

So, the only time he stopped working was in the hottest hour of the day to lay in the shade. Obie was starting to not ask, and part of Troylus felt bad. Not enough to change what he was doing, but it still sucked.

"What do I need to do today?" he asked, trying to get back to talking.

"Ummm…" Obie turned his head, bit his lip, and squinted at him like he was trying to come up with a good one this time. "How about you try flattening the ore this time."

"Are you sure you don't want me to forge it into steel for you?" Troylus shook his head, but Obie's eyes widened and a huge smile took over his face.

"Can you do that?"

"No, dumbass," Troylus said, ripping some of the stalks of grass and throwing them at him.

"Oh, well, what good are you then?"

They both laughed at that; they would be nowhere near as far along building the burgh as they already were after only a week if it weren't for Troylus using his ability until he ran out of it and collapsed for ten minutes.

"You know, you don't have to do it every single day. We'll build it faster than any other spindle at the rate we're going anyway, and I'm sure she'll wait."

"She will, I know that." And he did, Troylus didn't doubt Zellendine for a minute. "But I'm worried about her. After Briar…"

He didn't need to go on, everyone knew what had happened with Briar.

"I'm sure she's fine."

3

ZELLENDINE

SHE WAS NOT FINE. OF ALL THE NEW AND STRANGE THINGS ABOUT the reality of being on the planet, lugging supplies up and down the stairs that seemed to never end inside the spindle was one of the worst.

Her stomach ached, and her back was about to seize up in protest. The spasms in it were getting worse by the hour.

But she had work to do.

She finally reached the main level of the spindle and leaned against the railing for a second, letting go of the handles of the packages that left marks in her palms by the end of every day.

"Are you okay, Zellendine?" Imogene asked, pausing mid step, her arms laden with more suits for the starwalkers's first exit of the spindle.

"Yeah, I don't think I'm sleeping well yet. No big deal." She smiled and waved a hand, trying not to be the weak link for the day.

"None of us are sleeping yet, I don't think."

At the second she said it, another wave hit, the harsh

grinding noise that had become a regular occurrence shook the air and the entire spindle shuddered.

Imogene cringed and Zellendine shook her head; they both smiled as Imogene left to her task.

She was right, most of them weren't sleeping well with all the noise and the shuddering of the structure. It made Zellendine feel like shit, that everyone was going through the same difficulty, but she was the only one that seemed to be lagging behind.

A deep breath, and a grab for the damn handles, and she was back at work.

Two starwalkers were in the big service area getting food ready for the whole crew when she walked into the space and her patient was sitting on a bench at one of the long tables, their hand wrapped in a piece of fabric and resting on the table in front of them.

"What did you do this time?" she asked, plopping her stuff down beside Maurice.

He laughed and shrugged.

"I know why you were always on comms in the office when we were on the Wheel," she said, shaking her head.

The two guys cooking doubled over laughing at that.

She paused in unwrapping Maurice's hand from the fabric.

"Now you have to tell her how you did it," Corto, one of the guys, said.

Maurice blew a heavy breath through his lips and gave her a chagrined smile.

"I was in the office trying to hook up the comms so we could use them in here with headsets instead of the speaker system."

Of all the things that should have resulted in injury, she couldn't begin to imagine how him doing that would have.

Unwrapping his hand the rest of the way she discovered two cut fingers, one of them almost to the bone.

"How in the universe did you do that to yourself in an office?" she asked, grabbing a numbing cream first from one of her bags.

"It wasn't my fault," he said, and she rolled her eyes because she had heard that before. "Honestly, there was a ragged edge of the metal table at the back on the bottom and I was trying to see if I could run a hard cord, if maybe that would make it work better."

"But why were you at the back and underneath to run a hard cord? You could have just run it over the top of the table," she said, cleaning the wound so she could more accurately assess what she needed to do for it.

Maurice shrugged and the guys cooking laughed.

"Seemed like a good idea at the time," Maurice said.

"Remind me to tell the people coordinating the first mission outside not to let you be the first one out," she said, and even Maurice laughed at that.

"Don't worry, Zellendine, he has plenty of time to get himself stuck on bedrest between now and the first trip out," Corto said over his shoulder.

"Why? I thought all the supplies were ready and the terraforming was working," she said, and as if she had summoned it, the spindle around her shook and the noise that was starting to weave its way into her bones filled the air.

"Yeah," Maurice said, shaking his head and raising his brows after the noise stopped, "It's going well, but we're in the region that needs it the most. Terraformers told me that we're right next to some mountains and this place is so young there aren't rivers and streams at the bottom of the mountains, it's just a big soupy mess. They have to toughen up the land around us, because we're sinking."

"Sinking?" She tried to hold back the panic in her voice because she didn't know enough about the spindle or the way terraforming or building the burgh worked for panic to be warranted, but the thought of being stuck inside the spindle as it sank deeper and deeper into the planet made her stomach flip over and her breakfast want to make a reappearance.

"It's fine, they've got it under control. And besides, when it's all done, this might be the most beautiful burgh of them all, and we get the tunnels in the process which is just a cool bonus." Maurice's grin was an odd thing on his face. He was near the same age as Rullon, with a face more grizzled and less jowly, but his grin since they landed was like a child's, bright and unabashed.

"Are the tunnels staying? I thought they would dismantle them when it was all done," Corto said, starting to set things out on the long tables for everyone to have lunch.

"Yeah, I don't see anyone taking them apart. But who knows? This spindle won't be used like the others," Maurice said, reaching with his good hand for a plate, his whole body shifting to the side.

"Stop it. You have to wait until I'm done," Zellendine said, pulling on his arm to bring it back to directly in front of her.

"Come on," he complained.

"No, sit. Stay." She was focused solely on finishing up her work, but the laughter of the other people in their spindle as they filtered into the service still broke through her focus.

"I don't know, Maurice. I would maybe listen to the only person here who can patch you up every time you decide to hurt yourself." Imogene sat next to Zellendine, grabbed a plate, and started dishing up.

"One of us has to keep her busy," Maurice said and Zellendine shook her head.

"What I wouldn't give to be kept a little less busy," Zellendine said, putting the last of the bandage on Maurice's hand and collecting her scattered supplies back in her bags.

"Here." Imogene put a piled high plate in front of Zellendine, and she tried to smile at her in thanks, but her stomach was a roiling mass of anger at the very idea of food.

"Are you okay? Are we overworking you that much?" Maurice asked, stretching his hand toward her but not connecting, a gesture she was seeing among the crew more and more, the edicts of not touching starting to chafe.

"I'm okay, my stomach is a little upset, that's all." Zellendine put the last of her supplies away in her bags and turned back to the table, but all eyes were on her.

They were silent, some frozen with their hands holding their plates in the air, mid movement across the table.

"What?" she asked, her voice quiet, but they all had to have heard her in their silence.

"Do you think it's colony sickness?" Imogene asked, causing some of the others to cringe.

"No, I don't have a fever or any other symptoms," Zellendine said, and everyone started to breathe again, going back to their business.

But staring at the plate full of food she normally liked although it looked as appetizing as eating her uniform at that moment, she couldn't help but wonder, what if her body was rejecting being on the planet? What if she was developing colony sickness?

Every single plan she had, every single hope for her and Troylus and a future, depended on being on the planet.

If the planet itself was making her sick, where would they go from there?

She took a bite, her mouth salivating in the tight metallic way at the back of her throat as she chewed that gave her enough warning to leap from the table and sprint to the wet room.

After her stomach emptied of the little that was in it from

her morning meal, she stared at the remnants and hoped that whatever was wrong with her would go away soon.

Their spindle was deep in the planet, sinking by the day, terraforming in progress. It wasn't going to return to the ship and bring down more citizens, the other spindles would take care of that and some of those people would have to travel to the burgh they would build.

Even if she needed it, the spindle wasn't going to be able to take her back to the ship. And if it was colony sickness, the only way to survive was by going back to space.

"Please," she said, to the empty room, not even sure how to finish the sentence.

4

TROYLUS

He used every bit of his frustration and worry over Zellendine and their continued lack of comms to shove his ability at as much of the raw metal as possible, forcing it to flatten and form into the easily manipulated sheets they needed for the outside of the buildings.

Tendrils of blue light wove through the air, sheets of metal formed and flipped and stacked while his arms started shaking and sweat formed on his brow.

"Come on. We have to go faster," he said, his voice a growling version of how it normally sounded.

Every day it seemed like he had to push a little harder to get the same amount of production from his ability. And every day it left him even more exhausted when he was done.

With a stack of metal sheets, ready for them to use, and one in the air, pulling and whining, the sound exclusive to tortured metal, his ability started to slip.

He gritted his teeth, shutting his eyes against the glare of the sun beating down from overhead. Shoving, throwing all his desperation to get done faster, his need for news of Zellendine, his love, into the blue pouring from his hands, the light of it still dancing in shadowed brilliance through his eyelids, he finished the stack he wanted to. His body knowing when he was done and was allowed to let go even without his eyes seeing the world clearly before him, he fell over.

Landing on the ground, he smelled brittle grass, the dust tasted thick on his tongue, but the pain that should have been in his shoulder wasn't.

Somewhere in his head he heard the others calling his name, trying to get him to open his eyes, but he couldn't. Not yet. He couldn't understand why he wasn't in pain either.

One second he was standing, the next he was on the ground in a heap, most of his body was some level of numb, as if his brain and body just couldn't process any more information.

Maybe that's what it was. He couldn't think through it properly either.

It took time, less than an hour, but time, for him to come out of it completely.

"Hey, here," Obie said, holding a bottle of water out for him.

Troylus drank it down greedily, his entire body soaking it up as if he was the parched grass below him.

"You okay?" Obie asked, looking at the drained bottle and putting it in the satchel next to him.

"Where are we at now?" Troylus asked instead of answering, gesturing with his head to the construction he could hear just beyond Obie who was blocking his view.

"Making a lot of progress, but you're not done yet. Sorry." Obie leaned toward the noise of the others putting together the gathering room.

Or… at least that's the building Troylus thought they were working on. But that might have been the day before. He just needed to be done, he thought as he flopped onto his back on the ground, squinting up into the blue taking over from the angry colors of the sky.

"Does that mean the storm is clearing? Are we going to get comms?" he asked, trying not to jump up and run into the spindle to try them before he got an answer, or if he couldn't run, drag himself in there.

"Not yet, the storm is still going to take a while, but we think it's clearing. The real question is, what the hell is the weather pattern here when the storm is out of the mountains?" Obie picked at a piece of grass and threw the dust it crumbled into in the air, it wafted over them both, only adding to the layer of it already ground into their uniforms.

"Thanks for that," Troylus said, dusting at himself with a hand still weak enough to do little more than flop against his chest. He dropped it back to his side and looked up at the rocks of the mountain range in front of him. It was still amazing that this planet had naturally existing structures larger than the Wheel and all the spindles combined. He was taught that they existed, and that they might see them one day, but to experience their grandiosity in person… it left him in awe.

"Have you decided where you're going to settle with Zellendine and your family?" Obie asked, drawing Troylus from his own head.

"Indigo and Rullon haven't set foot on the planet yet. I'm assuming they'll be assigned wherever Zellendine and I decide to settle, but I want reports from all the burghs first." He flung an arm over his eyes to block some of the sun, but it didn't stop the sweat collecting in every dirt coated part of his body.

"Wherever we go, I'm hoping it won't be somewhere with no trees. This place is too dry and brown and too fucking hot," he said, Obie laughing before Troylus even got to the end, doubled over when he said hot.

"You would melt if you spent years here. And I don't think it would do you any good to bring her back here." Obie waved his hand in front of his nose and Troylus smiled.

"Okay, okay, I get it." Apparently a trip to the wash was in his future.

"How in the universe are you not even sweating?" Troylus asked, pulling his arm from his eyes and squinting at Obie.

"I said, I like it here. I was cold every day on the Wheel. For some reason, this kind of heat works for me. But it would be better if there was some rain once in a while to make the grass green." He stood up and walked to the rest of the people working on the building and Troylus wondered what they were going to do in this burgh when there was no way they would be able to grow their own food.

But he couldn't spend the time to care much about it, not when he needed to just focus on getting his ability energy stored back up so he could get to Zellendine faster.

"Zellendine," he said her name to the wind, hoping that whatever she was doing she knew he was trying. Whatever was happening in her spindle, he was going to find a way for his work to get done enough to get to her.

He sat up and shook out his hands and his feet like he was getting up from a stasis, a wry smile forming on his lips at the familiar movements from a thing he would never have to do again.

But… maybe.

He put the thought aside and headed on wobbly legs to help them build.

The evening in the region meant purple invaded the sky as the sun set behind the mountains, letting light slowly drain from the fields beyond the spindle.

For the first time since they came, everyone sat in the relative cool of the oncoming night, in the deeper shade of the spindle, while they ate their evening meal.

"So, what building is next?" one of the women asked, not for the first time. She was uniquely focused on getting to the houses, wanting to build a specific one for her own family that was waiting onboard the Wheel.

Troylus spotted one of the other crew members rolling their eyes, but he didn't mind her always asking when they would get to that point. He had a singular focus too.

Part of him had a hard time imagining himself in his pre-Zellendine focused head space being on the planet.

He wouldn't have been as productive, but it was more than that. Would he have even bothered to think about moving from his assigned burgh? He didn't think so, which made him look just a little closer at the place he was in.

Just beyond the edge of his clear sight there were shapes, large hulking black shapes looming above the tall grass.

"What are those?" he asked, the conversations around him quieting as he pointed.

The shapes were moving, a slow, meandering, patternless advance their direction.

"I can't see anything," Obie said beside him, squinting into the deepening darkness.

"Just past that change in the grass, where it's longer and darker in the daytime, there are animals of some kind out there I think," he said, leaning forward more.

"Should we go check it out?"

The others talked in hushed tones about the possibility of predators and threat, but most of them were still scanning the view as if they couldn't see what he was talking about.

One of the terraformers with them looked at him, silver eyes glinting, and nodded, proving to Troylus that his own eyesight was enhanced somehow from his ability, or maybe from the color change itself.

It didn't matter how, he wanted to use it. Otherwise, what good was having better abilities?

He got up from the group, quiet, and careful, the terraformer following behind him.

Everyone else was still discussing what other animals they thought they were going to encounter at some point. They knew there were some large ones on the planet, their scans had proved it, but they didn't believe they were sentient beyond the point the Chapter deemed too far advanced to colonize. That was all they knew.

For Troylus, it didn't seem like remotely enough to know.

And the Chapter wasn't trustworthy enough for him to believe much of what they had been told because it all seemed self-serving.

So he walked into the night in a half crouch, hoping to remain below the level of the tall grass and not spook whatever was out there, waiting for him.

5

ZELLENDINE

"NOTHING?" SHE ASKED, SITTING ON HER SMALL BED, IN HER makeshift quarters, the walls made up of blankets held up by stacked boxes at the corners with a blanket strung over the head of her bed so she could finally get some sleep.

"Sorry," Imogene said, scrunching her face up in sympathy as she stood at the end of the room with the blanket swept to the side like a sad, wilting door.

"Ragh," Zellendine grumbled, rubbing her face. "It's been weeks. He has to be losing his tether at this point."

"Kind of like you are?" Imogene's smile was gentle, but at that second, just looking at her silver eyes made Zellendine so frustrated not to be able to get word from Troylus that she could barely glance at her friend.

"Yes. I know. I'm dropping my handle." She laughed without humor and shook her head. "I just need some kind of word in or out. First, they thought it was the storm, but that isn't it. They can send word to the Wheel just fine, why not between our spindles?"

"We don't know. And I swear, we ask every time for word of

them, all we get are the reports." Imogene took the two steps needed for her to sit at the end of Zellendine's bed.

She had been doing it for a while, and Zellendine did the same in Imogene's room, but it still felt weird every time, like they were breaking protocol.

But this was the planet.

"Have you heard anything about when they think they're going to start bringing more people down?" she asked, trying to get back to other topics so she wouldn't scream.

"A few of the burghs are going up pretty quick so it shouldn't be too long for those places," Imogene said, her face transforming with a sly grin as she crossed her arms.

"What?" Zellendine squinted at her, not able to stop her mouth from turning up at the corners at the smug look on Imogene's face.

"I just thought you might find it interesting that of all the burghs, the one going up the fastest is Troylus's." She shrugged and glanced up, a huge smile breaking out on her face as Zellendine closed her eyes and took a deep breath, dropping her head back to look up at the blanket above her bed.

"So he's trying to get to me. That's what you mean," she said, making eye contact with Imogene who's smile only grew in response.

It was enough.

"Thank you. Really," she said and Imogene nodded.

"Do you know which burgh you think you're going to settle in? Will you stay here?" Imogene relaxed back into a more comfortable sitting position.

"Maybe" Zellendine leaned back against the shelf she used as the head of her bed, thinking about it. "I mean, we might stay in this area. It will depend on what he knows, what his region is like, what we hear about the other regions. But I do know we won't stay in a burgh."

"Where else would you live?" Imogene asked a line forming between her brows as she stared off into the middle distance like she was trying to come up with another possibility and failing.

"Back on the ship, we talked about building our own place, outside the burgh, somewhere with no Chapter influence on our lives and we would come into the burgh to trade for things we grew and made and maybe for me to give medic care when they needed more hands," she said with a shrug.

It was an imperfect plan, and by the line only deepening between Imogene's brows while she looked at her, she knew there were a lot more holes in it than she even realized. But it was their plan, and even just the thought of it made her happy.

"So it's just going to be you and Troylus out past the edge?"

"No. We'll bring Rullon, Indigo and her partner, and whoever else wants to go if there are any who do." Zellendine looked at Imogene as she said it, wondering if she would go with her.

But Imogene just stared back, giving away nothing of her thoughts on the possibility, and Zellendine decided it was better to just keep mentioning it instead of pushing.

"Well, I hope you're better by then," Imogene said, and as if on cue, Zellendine's stomach flopped and the back of her mouth started to water in that metallic way that told her it was going to happen again.

Jumping from the bed, Zellendine grabbed for the bowl she kept underneath it just for that reason, and lost part of her evening meal.

Imogene handed her a towel, the soft fabric hanging over her shoulder as she straightened up and tried to focus on what in the universe could be wrong with her, symptoms and diagnosis flying through her mind.

"Thank you. I'm sorry, this is so gross," Zellendine said,

taking the towel and wiping her face with it, draping it over the bowl when she was done.

"You're sure it's not colony sickness? There should be an answer by now," Imogene said, her shoes making a clear thudding as she walked up and down the tiny space behind Zellendine.

"Colony sickness has very specific symptoms, I've been monitoring myself for it, even checking my blood, and no. It's not that. But I can't find a thing that would explain it." She grabbed the bowl and stood on legs that were already more steady than they should be just post getting sick.

Making their way to the wet room with her nasty cargo, people they passed just glanced at the covered bowl and frowned before going about their own business. Everyone had become accustomed to her making the trip regularly. Which only made her feel worse.

"Do you think we should ask the medics on the ship? I mean, some of them have more experience, they might have an idea that you've never thought of," Imogene said once they were in the wet room as she looked away from Zellendine's process of cleaning up.

"But if I ask them, are they going to make me head back as soon as possible?" She didn't want anyone that close to leadership to know.

"And if you don't ask them, are you going to get worse?" Imogene asked, turning around to look Zellendine in the eye.

She didn't want to even think about getting worse, she was getting sick randomly all through the day and felt like she was hungry, sore, and tired all the time, but she couldn't ignore the reality that Imogene made some sense.

"How about I let them know if I get worse?"

Imogene opened her mouth like she was going to argue, but

Zellendine lifted her brows and Imogene smiled instead with a tilt of her head.

"Listen, that's a good suggestion to ask for more diagnostic help, but I am handling this. In fact, my body has adjusted to whatever is going on by making me hungrier, so clearly it's trying to heal itself. Let's just give it a chance before we involve leadership."

They stared across the room at each other, neither one of them moving, and Zellendine's heart sped up.

If Imogene wanted to, she could include the information about the sickness in the reports and send it to the ship without Zellendine even knowing. But all she could do was try and trust that her friend wouldn't do that to her. That she would trust her to know if that step was needed or not.

Finally, Imogene nodded and Zellendine's shoulders relaxed.

"But," Imogene said, and Zellendine's heart hammered away at the inside of her chest, "If we get comms through to Troylus's spindle, I am telling him."

Zellendine opened her mouth to argue, but Imogene held up a hand to stop her.

"You would want to know if it was the other way around."

She would have, but…

"Imogene, if he finds out, he'll come totally untethered. He'll find a way, anyway, to get here. Even if it hurts him to do it."

"He might not, it might just be one more reason for him to work hard and make it to you, he might even be able to get some insight from his own medic."

The smile that formed on Zellendine's face was one of equal parts longing and pride, "No. He will drop his handle. I know. Because it's what I would do."

6

TROYLUS

The animals were huge. Larger than he even realized when he first noticed them.

He crouched in the grass, spying on them through the tall, thin stalks.

It wasn't just the distance that made their movements look slow and seemingly without pattern. The animals had four legs, their whole bodies covered in dark, long hair, with large sloped backs, and huge heads with long gnarled horns above their ears.

"What are they?" he whispered into the wind.

But the wind was more likely to answer him than any of his people. A whole new world meant all new animals and all new names for them.

Among the things he did know, was that they were not predators. Form followed function according to what he was taught, which meant that the animals grazing in front of him, taking no notice of his presence, with their eyes on either side of their massive heads, no matter that there were six eyes in total, were prey animals.

Which left him with the question, what preyed on beasts as large as they were?

Taking the chance, Troylus stood up.

One of the animals lifted its head, all three eyes on that side staring at him as it continued to chew. Its big mouth moved in a lazy, rounded bite pattern. The other animals around stopped moving, continued with their heads down to chew, but none of them took steps in their meandering way.

Troylus's heart was as loud inside his head as the animals were huge, but he heard the humming sounds that passed back and forth between the creatures. The one eyeing him did the most humming, a low, undulating bass sound that Troylus felt as much as he heard.

Long minutes went by with neither human nor creature changing their position.

Part of him wanted to really see what the animals would do, part of him wanted to get closer. But he measured with his eyes and decided that their defenses were greater than anything he wanted to test. His ability wasn't likely to help him when he didn't have much around him to use. Well, at least he wasn't ready to test the theory yet.

Instead, Troylus moved away. One step at a time he backed up. The only hint that the animals were even aware of his movements was the slight change in the vacillating pattern of the beast's humming.

Finally, he was beyond the tall grass and the one watching him tilted its head back to get another bite.

He turned and made his way to the others sitting by the spindle.

"Well, that was stupid as shit," Obie said as he sat down amongst the others.

"It was fine." Troylus was more than fine as he stared into

the dark, the light too far gone for him to still see the animals anymore.

"You didn't know that when your fool ass went out there." Obie shook his head and Troylus smiled.

"No, but they aren't predators, they're prey animals of some kind. And they're massive. We should probably let the other spindles know as soon as we can get word to them that there might be a very large predator on this planet."

"Oh, you think?" Obie rolled his eyes and everyone laughed.

The terraformer who went out there with Troylus told everyone of his observations while Troylus looked up at the stars peeking through the veil of the night sky.

Be careful, Zellendine, he thought.

Among the dry grass covered plains spread out before him had to be far more animals than he was aware of. If the region was rich enough to support the size of animals that those were, it could support a rich and varied flora and fauna. He just needed to pay more attention.

"Even after seeing those things you're still planning on walking to her aren't you?" Obie asked sometime later when the conversations about the animals had died down.

"Yes." He didn't bother to try and hide his intentions, he didn't bother to try and explain for the thousandth time why heading back to the Wheel on a spindle and then waiting more until he could catch one going to her region was not an option.

"I should already be gone," he said, his voice floating away on a breeze so no one heard it but him.

Obie rubbed his hands over his face and dropped them while he shook his head. The consternation on his face was mirrored on the others around them but Troylus just shrugged.

"So, we can't talk this one out of his bad idea, let's all come up with some bad ideas of our own," Obie said, grinning.

"What does that even mean?" Troylus asked, earning laughter from some of the others.

"New animal, right?" Obie asked, gesturing at the dark in the general direction of where they were.

"And?"

"And, we need to come up with names for them."

People started to groan and Troylus laughed as he looked back up at the sky. There would be a lot of new animals and seven new burghs to name. The list was daunting and he was glad it wasn't up to him.

"Noonoo?" someone on the other end asked, their voice shrill and cracking on the laugh they couldn't contain.

"What's a noonoo?"

"That's what this idiot wants to name a giant thing with horns. A bird, sure, but that big beast?" The laughter was a sharp peal in the night and Troylus just shook his head as he smiled.

"How does it make more sense for a bird?"

"You all know that it doesn't matter what we name everything, half of our ideas are going to be made fun of for generations, it's the way of names," he said, and by the time he was done he had to sit up and look down the line of his crew members because they had all fallen silent.

"No pressure, huh, Troylus?" one of the others at the end yelled and it broke the spell, causing everyone to laugh again.

"Serious question, though." He raised his hand and they all quieted enough to hear what he had to say again. "How in the universe do parents ever pick their kid's name?"

"Don't ask me, my parents sucked at it," Obie said and the group was back to laughter and terrible ideas for names of animals.

7

ZELLENDINE

Imogene shook her shoulder to wake her up.

Zellendine wiped at her face, trying to force her eyes open and her brain into gear.

"Sorry, this is embarrassing now," Zellendine said, her words still not clear as she took in the fact that she was leaning next her plate at the table near service.

"I fell asleep again?" she asked, the others were doing the last of the cleanup from their meal and her plate looked almost clear so she at least ate first that time.

"You need to do another full test panel on yourself," Imogene said, the line back between her brows and deeper than it had ever been.

"Come on," Zellendine said, getting up from the table and bringing her dishes to the crew members still cleaning up.

"Right now." Imogene's voice behind her was hard, like she was gearing up for the fight that bubbled up inside Zellendine.

"No." Zellendine grabbed her bags from the table and headed to the medic bay, an alcove really that held all her back up supplies.

"You can't keep saying no." Imogene followed her, tight on her heels, their steps ringing out in that hollow echoey way that sharp sounds did in the open space of the main part of the spindle.

"And you can't keep following me. I'm fine." Zellendine shoved her bags into one of the cupboards, upsetting a scanning stand and sending it toppling to the floor in the harsh clang of metal on rock.

"What the fuck is this floor made of?" she yelled, grabbing the stand and setting it right before slamming the door of the cupboard shut.

"I don't know. All the spindles are very old." Imogene's voice was irritating in its calm which only made Zellendine angrier.

"Thanks for using that voice, now I look like an asshole," she said, shooting Imogene a glare when she only blinked back at her.

"How is the tone of voice I use a reflection on you?" Imogene asked and Zellendine threw up her hands as she stormed off.

Because anyone listening would think she had dropped the handle completely and was angry for no reason. And she didn't have the excuse of her eyes turning silver to fall back on for her attitude. When Troylus and the others were so full of rage there was a reason, even if it still didn't entirely make sense to her, she knew it existed. But her emotions weren't caused by anything that she understood. Just that the last thing she wanted to do was risk being put back on the ship.

She didn't go to her tiny curtained room. She didn't want to be alone even though she wasn't sure she really wanted to be around anyone else either.

There was one person she wanted to see. One person who she thought she wouldn't have been angry with even in the vulnerable place she found herself. It was time she tried to see about the comms herself.

In the large, open space of the main portion of the spindle, in the middle of the round room, was a hole. She made her way to the stairway at the edge of it, leaning against the railing to look down into the depths of the many levels.

Lights shone from the different levels to illuminate the hole that the stairs wrapped around and around.

She hated the stairs. Metal things with rough grating and holes that the light shone through, they made the thought of falling on them terrifying in their fierceness.

At least on that trip down she was able to hang onto the rail with both hands. Normally she was over loaded with her bags and had to navigate the stairs without the help of hanging onto anything but her nerve.

Her hands around the railings, she went floor after floor, deeper into the spindle toward the floor of their main controls and comms equipment.

Finally, her legs aching, her heart thudding, and her breaths dragging in and out, she made it to the same floor they were all on when they arrived.

The straps that held her when they landed, and those that held the others, hung from their places along the walls, looking for all the universe no more important than her hanging wall curtains.

She ran her fingers along the straps and wondered if she would ever be able to look at them as anything less than the magical articles of her deliverance from the Chapter. It made her want to slice a piece off and take it with her.

But if she was to make good on the chance the straps had afforded her and make it away from the burghs and the spindles, she didn't need to mess with Chapter property.

The main board which the comms things were on was not what she was used to dealing with. But there had to be a way to get it to work between the spindles. It just didn't make sense for there to be no way to send messages between themselves. Just for safety purposes it was important.

Maybe if they weren't half buried in the planet and actively terraforming the region around them, maybe then they would be able to get their comms to work properly.

She stood up straight, looking around and taking in all the equipment, trying to discern which things were specifically for comms.

Darting back to the stairs, she leaned over the railing, looking down further into the engineering floors and up toward the main space.

Running back up the stairs, her legs told her was a mistake. They weren't used to being used in the way that the stairs required, it sent pain through her muscles that threatened to seize them up.

Her breath moved in ragged, harsh sounding gasps in and out and she tried to keep her focus on her footing, but her mind wandered to whether it would work, and if it did, would she be able to see and hear Troylus.

Almost there, she was almost to the main floor, the hole expanding to the large ceiling filled with constant light drew closer with every sharp stab of pain in her muscles.

She missed a step.

In a desperate grab at the railing she caught it with one hand, the other sliding between the rails as she toppled toward the metal grate of the stair treads.

Zellendine screamed, a short, sharp sound, cut off instantly when her head collided with the metal.

8

TROYLUS

"How far out here are we planning to go?" Obie asked, adjusting the pack on his back and holding a hand to his eyes to shield them from the sun still barely up on the horizon.

"As far as we need to." Troylus closed his eyes and let the sun soak into him as he walked. It was different than in the heat of the day, in the still cool of the morning the light was energizing and refreshing.

"You don't even know for sure if we're heading in the right direction," Obie said at the ground, his voice petulant and quiet.

He decided he didn't need to poke at Obie, dragging him out there was good enough.

The guy said he wanted to stay in the region, but he was weirdly attached to the confines of the burgh for a starwalker. He needed to get out, Troylus thought, smiling to himself and giving Obie a sidelong glance.

By the time he left, Obie was going to hate him. It took everything in him not to laugh out loud at his own thoughts. Sometimes it was fun to be an ass, even if he was only doing it in his thoughts.

"Why do you want to see them so bad?"

"I think we should all know who our neighbors are going to be, especially when they're huge and we should probably know more about their patterns," he said, stepping around a heaping, stinking pile of dung.

"Gross, it would also help us know to look for giant shit pits so we don't step in them," Troylus said, wrinkling his nose and waving a hand in front of his face.

"That's nasty. A shit pit? What are you, twelve?" Obie asked, but there was laughter again in his voice and his pace picked up.

"Oh, to be twelve again." Troylus thought back to the ages when he spent every day with Zellendine, hanging out in trees in the orchard and stealing snacks. But Briar was with them too.

His memories were clouded by what had happened since.

"Never mind," he mumbled and Obie squinted his eyes at him.

"What's the matter?"

"I… Obie, if you were in love with someone, and they were talking about partnering with someone else who you cared about but knew wasn't right for them, and you decided to kiss that person, how much of a dick would you be?" Troylus knew that his friend was staring at the side of his head, he could feel the gaze boring into his soul.

"Are we talking about the same guy that tried to kill her?" Obie asked, the tone of his voice dark and heavy.

"Yeah, but that was later. That was because of the ability, for some reason she's a big target of the anger it causes." Troylus waved a hand, trying to think through how messed up he was over Briar, why he felt guilty that Briar was on the ship when he made the case himself that Briar should have been able to fight the rage.

"Troylus, when you were pissed off at her, did you ever come close to swinging on her?" Obie grabbed his arm and stopped his forward momentum.

He took a deep breath and shook his head.

"No." Troylus started walking again, knowing Obie was as right as he was when he said it on the ship. But still, he couldn't help glancing to the sky, to the Wheel hanging in space just beyond the atmosphere.

"Maybe I just feel like I stole his life," Troylus said, his voice hushed and his throat going dry.

"That's just stupid." Obie walked past him, his eyes on the grass in front of himself, so he couldn't have seen the smile that formed on Troylus's face.

But maybe he knew anyway.

Ahead of them, a humming started, the same rumble that moved through Troylus's body the night before.

He grabbed Obie by the arm and turned him to face him, his other hand holding a finger over his own mouth.

Obie's eyes widened a fraction and he looked around after he nodded.

Picking his steps carefully, Troylus moved through the grass, trying in vain not to send the sound of crackling grass through the air with each footfall.

But the animals didn't stir beyond the humming sound.

He parted one last bushel of tall grass and uncovered the big beasts laying on the ground. Their legs looked like they were no longer there under the long hair of their hide. All of them looked like they were sleeping, but he suspected none of them were. The big one from the night before was right in front of him.

It's three eyes facing him blinked, their pupils a light brown that sparkled in the light as if there was gold in them.

Troylus crouched down in front of the animal, his face level with the eyes while the long horn was above his head.

Fear should have paralyzed him as it seemed like it had Obie behind him. But though his heart hammered in his chest and he took careful, slow breaths, his hand didn't shake as he reached out to touch the course, short hair on the creature's face.

It blinked, a long, slow closing of its eyes, the humming from within it changing to only a soft murmur, and when it opened its eyes again, Troylus didn't know why he knew it wasn't going to hurt him. But he did.

"You're just big, huh?" he whispered, his voice quiet and low and still sounded harsh to him among the incredible hum that moved through him from the animal.

"We're not going to hurt you. I just wanted you to know. And if you know of any mean things out there, give us a heads up, yeah?"

The giant head dipped a fraction, and the eyes blinked. Troylus took it as a yes, or as close as he was going to get.

He stood, inch by inch, the muscles in his legs wanting to cramp half way up when he was at eye level with the thick, gnarled horn, but he made it to standing without the beast even giving a twitch of disagreement. He backed away, not sure what the protocol would be when he was meeting a foreign and wild species, but it seemed like a good idea.

By the time the long grass moved back into place to shield him from the view of the many eyed creatures, he turned and headed back toward the spindle, more than ready to exhaust himself working toward getting the burgh done.

"Are you untethered?" Obie asked as he passed him, turning to trail after him.

"Nope. But now you all don't have to worry about those giant things and maybe they won't have to worry about a bunch of people getting freaked out by their presence and hurting them either."

"What the fuck are you?" Obie asked, his voice hushed and quavering.

Troylus looked over at him and broke out in laughter.

"Seriously? Those things have six eyes, and you're asking me what I am?"

It took a second. Obie continued to stare at him, open mouthed, but eventually the corners of his lips flicked up and soon he was laughing along with Troylus.

But even though they walked back laughing and chatting, Troylus couldn't help but wonder at his friend's question.

He was on a different planet than the one his father was born on, that one a different planet than the one his father was born on, and so on back generations. He had abilities that didn't make sense for humans, he had markers in his DNA and his blood that were different, even from what he had been born with.

The changes came before he got to this world, but maybe they made him belong on this place. Maybe he wasn't quite human anymore.

And if he wasn't all human anymore, what was he? And what did that mean for the other people from the ship? Especially the ones like Zellendine who showed no signs of changing.

9

―――

ZELLENDINE

She blinked in and out of consciousness, every time she came to, a sharp pain pierced through her head and her arm screamed at her until the world around her went black again.

Flashes of the main room went by, her body weightless and moving. It took more than a few moments of coming back to clarity for her to realize she was being carried.

Eyes flying open, she leaned to the side and vomit poured out of her mouth to drip on the floor.

A voice above her said her name.

Someone cursed the universe.

Crashing sounds invaded her mind.

Finally, she was stationary, Imogene's silver eyes just out of focus and beyond them, the alcove of the medic station.

Zellendine tried to move a hand, to indicate where the medication was that she thought she needed, but her arm didn't move. Instead, searing, excruciating pain ricocheted up her limb and through her side.

She screamed.

The world went black, but when it blinked back into existence for her, she still heard screaming.

TROYLUS

HIS BLUE LIGHT WRAPPED AROUND THE METAL, FLATTENING IT into as many sheets as he could manage at once, the sweat of his brow dripped into his eye. He squeezed it shut and kept pushing. Shoving every bit of his frustration over the lack of word, every bit of his heart ache at missing Zellendine, and every bit of the wonder of the planet that had become his constant companion, he used it all until he toppled to the side and caught himself with a knee in the dirt.

The blue light sputtered, but he gritted his teeth and kept on. He forced the metal to finish the work he set out to do with it and he fell to the side, sprawling out on the ground.

Sunlight, filtered through his lids, was golden and warm.

Every breath tasted of dust and exhaustion.

But there was a level of contentment, small though it was, he was so close to done with his work on the burgh. He was so close to going to his new home.

All he had to do was one more day's worth of work, and figure out the comms issue so he could coordinate how he was going to get there. To her.

"Comms are up," Obie yelled from close to the spindle, but Troylus could only sit up and blink at him. He must have been hallucinating. There was no way they were fixed while he was daydreaming about them being fixed.

"What?" He asked, his voice probably not loud enough to carry to Obie standing in the doorway and bouncing like he wanted to sprint back inside.

"Troylus, comms. Now." He turned and ran, leaving Troylus to scramble to his feet on legs made of boneless rope and a body that screamed at him to lay the fuck back down.

"Are they talking to her?" His voice bounced off the metal spindle next to him to reverberate back every drop of the panic in it and amplify it, sending the hairs on his arms skyward.

Other crew members called out to him as he stumbled and ran inside. He didn't bother to even turn back to look at them, let alone answer. They would find out eventually, but he had to get to the comm.

Need spurred him forward, there was no thought to the damage he might do to himself as he rammed into a corner of a wall and bounced off.

He made it to the stairs and climbed the two floors to where the comms room was as fast as his half dead legs would fly up the steps. The rhythmic nature of the steps was the only thing that saved him a fall because he didn't bother to put out his hands to the railing, it might have slowed him down.

Running, a cramp forming somewhere in one of his thighs, he careened into the back of one of the crew that was crowded around the comms.

Someone's hands caught him before he bounced off to slam into the floor with his knees, but his eyes were on the holo of the comm.

"Is she there? Are you talking to her spindle?" he asked, his voice hoarse as he tried to breathe through the words.

"Troylus?" It wasn't Zellendine's voice coming through, but it was one he knew.

"Maurice?" he asked, dragging himself on his knees to the table, not bothering to take the time to stand up.

"Oh, thank the universe," Maurice said, but the holo was just waving lines and spiking fractals, he couldn't see anything. So they still didn't have everything fixed.

"Where is Zellendine?" he asked, the faces of the people around him only then registering as they all averted their eyes from him and the comm.

"Troylus, it's Imogene," Imogene said on the other end.

In all their panicked last moves on the Wheel he didn't realize Zellendine was assigned the same spindle as her.

"Come on, Imogene, where is she?" He felt like he could breathe a little easier with her there for Zellendine, but they had to be bringing her to talk to him. Why was it taking so long?

"She's hurt. It's really bad. And she's our only medic."

The air around him was gone, her words sucked it all away and left him gasping.

"Get her back to the Wheel," he screamed, his voice cracking.

"We can't. We're too deep and our terraforming isn't good enough yet for another spindle to land here. All we can do is give her pain medication." The comm blinked and Troylus slammed his fists, emptied of their ability to even try and fix it, against the table top, leaving him hanging on it with his entire upper body.

"No. You have to do something. Have one of the medics on the Wheel talk you through what you need to do." His voice was harsh and jagged, like he had transformed into shattered glass.

"Troylus," she said, her voice quiet and the sadness of it tore his heart to shreds. "There's nothing we can do. She fell down a flight of stairs."

He turned his head back toward the stairs he had just

sprinted, he couldn't even see them through the press of bodies, but he didn't need to. In his mind he saw her falling against the unforgiving metal grate of the identical steps in her spindle.

"It's her brain, Troylus. I'm so sorry."

Without him, she was going to slowly slip away without him. There was no way he could get to her in time, and his hands, his ability was one of the only ways to save her. He knew it, deep in him, that if he was there, he could have healed her with a touch.

"Zellendine," he said to the air, wondering if they could even bring her to the comm, and if they could, would she hear him.

"Maybe…" he said, his voice trailing off as the medic on his crew spoke to Imogene on the other end, asking her questions and getting gruesome detail in response about the blood and the mangled section of her head.

"Imogene," he interrupted, the others stopping their conversation in a second at his wail of her name.

"Yes? I'm here, Troylus," she said, her voice full of trepidation.

"On the Wheel, I could fix people too, not just the ship. So can you," he said and multiple, sudden intakes of breath around him sounded like hissing.

"Troylus, I'm not sure that's a good idea. I've never even tried it."

He could practically hear her shaking her head.

"No, you can. I know you can. If I can, you can. All you have to do is tap into the same emotion when you're fixing something and focus on wanting to fix her."

"I don't think…"

"Please." His crumbled heart hammered away inside his chest, not swift or unsteady, but hard and forceful. Each beat seemed to take a millennia and it hit so hard the echo of the hurt it caused moved through his entire body.

"Please," he said again, tears streaming from his eyes, dripping off his chin and landing on the comms table.

"But…"

He squeezed his eyes shut, so tight it was painful, but the tears didn't stop and his mouth didn't stop forming the word please.

"I…"

"Please."

"What if I hurt her?" Imogene's voice was so small he could barely hear her, but her words let him take in a shuddering breath.

"You won't. At this point, you're the only chance she has. The only chance I have. Please, Imogene, just try." His tears splashed against the table to splatter back on his arms, but he couldn't move. Not until she agreed.

"Okay. I'll try. But please don't be angry with me if it doesn't work."

BRIAR

THE SHIP TURNED AND THE EDGE OF THE PLANET CAME INTO VIEW through the window. Briar balled his fists in his lap.

"I'm not sure these outings will continue if you can't learn to school your face," Grandpa Kason said, sitting next to Briar and watching out the window with him.

"Part of my sentence is that I get to be let out once in a while, are you changing that all on your own?" Briar asked, his voice as low and steady as the old man's, but his fists were still tight and his body still held too still.

"What I might be changing is what I advocate for when leadership meets again."

Briar's face might have shown too much, but anyone's would have in comparison to the craggy mask next to him.

"You said yourself, I should be down there, not them." He wanted to scream, he wanted all the people scattered around the gathering room to watch as the ship turned by the planet to hear him. He wanted them all to understand that it should have been him down there. More than most, certainly more than the traitors, he should have been among the first to claim the planet for the Chapter.

"And I also said that, because of what happened, no one will agree to that yet." Grandpa turned from the rich green of the planet as it came further into view and looked directly at Briar.

He waited until Briar turned back to him and their eyes were locked on each other.

"We need to be careful now, Briar. I need you to think about the long term goal of the Chapter."

Briar didn't know why Grandpa Kason's eyes hadn't turned silver. He wasn't immune, he knew that much, his body could tell. But every time he looked at the old man, agreed to take directions from him, part of him balked because he should have been listening to someone who was fully accepted by their new world.

Still, he forced himself to nod.

"I know the long term goal, and I am a good citizen of the Wheel," he said, as if he was small and still learning the protocols and the culture of the ship even though he was the person on the ship who understood how to be a dedicated citizen more than anyone else on board.

Grandpa Kason nodded and turned back to look out the window.

"Eventually, we will need to address the problem," he said, turning back to the window himself while Grandpa Kason froze next to him.

"How are you suggesting we address the problem?"

"The traitors need to be dealt with, even if we have to do it quietly and away from a burgh." The burghs, he squeezed his fists even tighter to stop the flames that wanted to burst from him. He was a terraformer, he was supposed to be down there, helping one of those teams build the burghs.

"Anything else?"

Briar scanned the room, trying to determine who among the people, in their little groups, was immune like Zellendine was. Maybe only one person in the room sent his body wanting to burst into flames and attack, but he wasn't sure if he was missing some of them or not.

"If the people who are immune are allowed to remain on the planet with the rest of us, it will only lead to more fights. They shouldn't be allowed to settle there. And the ones that are already down there…" He didn't finish the sentence, by the quick jerk of Grandpa Kason's eyes to him and back to the window, he thought the old man understood.

The planet, their new world, had spoken. It had changed him and all the others with silver eyes so they knew who they had to exclude.

"Some people are accepted, some aren't," he said. "That isn't our fault or even their's. It just is, and in order to keep moving forward, we need to make sure that the Chapter no longer includes the people who aren't acceptable to our planet."

Grandpa Kason cleared his throat and dropped his head, looking into his lap.

"What you're talking about, that's a lot of people."

"Yes, but it's needed." Briar nodded to himself, there was no doubt in him. He was as sure of the fact that the planet only wanted some people to settle it as he was of the fact that Stephen and Zellendine were traitors and he made a mistake in testifying for her.

"How exactly do you think we could ever expel people from the Chapter though?" Grandpa Kason delivered his words to his lap, his weathered face hanging and managing to make him look even more aged. "Why wouldn't we just give them supplies, a spindle, and coordinates to another planet they could settle on their own?"

"Because," Briar said, a smile on his face because Grandpa

Kason would agree with him, he was sure of it, "This planet has rejected them. We shouldn't waste our own precious supplies and a spindle on people who shouldn't move through the universe. I don't know what they did, but it was something."

Grandpa Kason slowly raised his head, his eyes tight, as he stared at Briar.

"You really believe that." It wasn't a question, and Briar was more than happy to say that he did, it was the only thing that made sense.

"Of course I do. We will probably never know what all the immune did to earn the planet's disfavor, but it had to be something fundamentally wrong, not just the normal human mistakes. The planet has given us a chance to rid ourselves of people who are not worthy of the Chapter."

"Why do you keep saying it's the planet? We don't actually know what caused all the abilities to show up, and according to the medics it has something to do with radiation."

"The planet, the sun, the galaxy, does it matter what gave us this tangible thing to point out the unworthy among us?" Briar's fists finally unfurled, Grandpa Kason was taking to his idea, he was sure of it.

If Briar could get Grandpa Kason to agree with him, he had a much better shot at getting all of leadership with him on the cause. If that happened, then he could be the perfect citizen he had always wanted to be, and he would get the chance to punish Zellendine for her treachery. Maybe he could become a hero to his people.

He hoped that they would all know what he had to endure to do what needed done. Someone like him should never have been locked up, least of all for months while he missed the beginning of the settling.

"Briar," Upton's small voice yelled from the doorway as his little brother ran toward him.

"No, sorry," Grandpa Kason said, shoving an arm between Briar and the advancing boy.

"I just want to talk to him." Upton turned from Grandpa Kason with his overly concerned face to Briar, the strange aging that had come over his features, not entirely gone when he looked at his brother.

"Are you coming back to our quarters now?" Upton asked as Journo came up behind him.

"No. He isn't done serving his sentence yet. I was trying to get him to focus on the planet so it could help inspire him in the hard work of rehabilitation." Grandpa Kason nodded to Journo and Upton as he levered himself to standing.

"Oh, so I'm not allowed to say, I miss you and hope you get better soon so you can come live with us again." Upton looked at Grandpa Kason as he spoke, which was probably a good thing because he missed how hard it was for Briar not to laugh.

"Don't worry," Journo said, looking at his eldest son, "I'm sure he'll get the message."

"We have to return him to his quarters now," Grandpa Kason said, gesturing to Briar who stood and followed him, but the message had come through.

And to him, it meant that he needed to play along so he could get out of there faster, because he needed to protect his little brother from the immune and the traitors.

It wasn't just a theory in his head anymore, it was need.

TROYLUS

HE PACED BACK AND FORTH, THE COMM CONNECTED TO Zellendine's spindle letting out a low buzz as the people on the other end had abandoned it and not closed it.

"Did they really all have to go see if it would work?" Obie asked one of the people on their own comm who just shrugged.

But Troylus knew why.

"It was Maurice and Imogene, they're my friends and hers. Plus," his voice broke and he took a deep breath, "it's Zellendine. Trust me, she's easy to love."

He swallowed, hard, wrung his hands together in front of himself and started pacing again.

"Why don't we try and get some food in you while we wait," Obie said, coming to pace alongside him.

"You go ahead. I'm staying right here until I know something." Troylus didn't even look at Obie who stopped pacing and went back to sit down near one of the chairs, leaning on the leg of the table.

"Maybe you could sit down. You used all your energy out there. You have to be exhausted."

But he wasn't. Not anymore.

He shook his head and turned back around, his feet pounding out the seconds that took too damn long.

"Troylus," their own medic, Xander, asked, "what if it only partially works?"

"I don't know what you mean," he said, his voice gruff and harsh as he choked down tears and tried not to scream at the man because thinking about the possibility of it not working was not what he needed.

"You have less ability every day." His voice was gentle, but Troylus's feet still stuttered a step before he closed his eyes and resumed his pattern.

"No. This will work."

"But if it only partially works, she may have to go back to the Wheel for further treatment. She may never be the same."

Troylus rounded on Xander, his hands gripped each other so tight his knuckles popped.

"Please stop talking," he said, his voice like a punch, even to his own ears.

Xander cringed and looked away.

Putting his hands to his face and rubbing, hard, against his eyes, he shoved his fingers through his hair and kept walking.

Minutes that felt like hours went by, his feet pounded, his heart thudded against his chest, his lungs ached with each breath as his mind shoved away the repeated thought that every time he took in air it would be the last time she did.

The crew members gathered around the comms whispered amongst themselves as he screamed inside his own mind to drown out anything they said.

He put his hands on his head, weaving his fingers into his hair until the pain of it pulling made his eyes water over something other than the thought of losing her.

"Just be okay." His words weren't directed at anything, just let go into the universe in the hope that she would somehow feel it, feel him.

"Imogene is trying," Obie said, his voice quiet, like he was testing talking to him again.

Nodding his head, his hands still wrapped in his own hair, Troylus paced again.

"Yes, but I need to be there. I…" Tears made their way onto his cheeks again, his eyes burned as they fell. "I'm not there, I can't help her."

"Troylus, this isn't your fault."

But wasn't it? If they had partnered, then he would have been there, he could have helped her. His mind went through every way in which he hadn't done enough for her, been enough for her. It was a sick skill, he decided, the ability to see every mistake he had ever made when it was too late to do anything about them.

"On the ship we put people into space, what do we do on the planet?" someone asked, their whisper, barely audible, made it to his ears and he collapsed to his hands and knees.

In the process of falling, he tore his hands out of his hair, taking strands of it with them, they were all he could focus on as he stared down at his hands braced on the floor.

"What the fuck?" someone else said to the whisperer.

Troylus dragged in searing breath after searing breath and wanted to get the thought out of his head. He didn't want to remember when he stood next to her as she watched her father go through the chute. He didn't want to remember when he watched others go to the stars. He didn't want to remember dragging all the bodies in after the accident.

She might already have become just a body. She might have already been gone, a beautiful, empty vessel with her blonde hair marred by blood and trauma.

He choked on a sob and bent his head to his hands not the floor.

Fighting back the tears, he shoved himself back to standing and shook his head at Obie who had come to his side.

If anyone got too close to him, or if any of them touched him, he was going to break down completely, and Zellendine deserved for him not to give up on her.

Pacing, he went back to pacing, swiping at his eyes and the damn tears that wouldn't stop.

"Come on, Imogene. Come on," he said, not sure if he was asking her to hurry up and give him an update, or if he was asking her to heal Zellendine, or both.

"Troylus?" Maurice's voice crackled over the comm and he dove for the table, slamming into it with his hip and bracing himself with a hand on either side of the messed up holo.

"I'm here. I'm here. How is she?" His words melded into one he spoke so fast, but he just swiped the tears away again and held his breath instead of trying to say anything else.

"Zellendine isn't all the way healed," Maurice said and Troylus's legs gave out. "Imogene did all she could and passed out. It only lasted a second and when she came to, she said she'll do it again every day until she's all the way better."

"How bad? Maurice, is she going to last until Imogene can help her again? How bad is she now?" His voice edged toward a wail, if the news was that he was going to lose her before Imogene could try again, he was going to scream, it waited in his chest.

"I just sent you the report from the scan. None of us really know how to read it. The medics on the Wheel taught us how to run it, but we can't tell what it says."

Xander fumbled with the comm buttons, he tapped away at the screwed up holo and it changed to the kinds of files that was used to seeing Zellendine work through.

He squeezed his eyes shut, it was too much. Looking at it wouldn't tell him anything either, other than the fact that he never wanted to see another one unless he was looking at it over Zellendine's shoulder.

"Um…" Xander said, shooting a glance at Troylus with his mouth hanging open.

"What?" Troylus shouted, grabbing onto Xander's arm, "Is she going to live? Will she last long enough for Imogene to keep helping her?"

"Yes. I think Imogene healed a lot, and I'm sure continued attention will help her a lot… it's just…" He looked back at the holo, tapping at it, switching from piece to piece, looking at things more than once.

"It's just what?" Maurice yelled on the other side of the comm.

"She… I didn't think this was possible, but it had to have happened on the ship for her to be this far along." Xander tapped at something else and shook his head.

"What happened on the ship? Complete sentences," Troylus said, ready to shove Xander out a chute, seriously thinking that flying the spindle back to the ship in orbit to do it might have been worth it.

"Zellendine is pregnant."

1 3

ZELLENDINE

SHE BLINKED IN AND OUT, SOMETHING ABOUT A SKULL FRACTURE, something about brain damage and swelling.

But she couldn't think clear enough to process the words. When the light was there, all she wanted was for it to go away and leave her in the dark.

In the dark she didn't feel pain. In the dark there wasn't shouted, panicked words.

Deep in the dark of her own mind, she was with Troylus, his arms around her, asleep in the bed they shared for too little a time, Rullon snoring in the other bunk.

The light was jarring, the pain whole, encompassing her entirely.

Her dark was soft, inviting, warm. And she wanted to stay.

14

TROYLUS

"IT DOESN'T MATTER," HE SAID, SHOVING ANOTHER HANDFUL OF bars into the pack.

"Yes. It does. Leadership will be fucking livid," Obie said.

"Why? If they had listened when we said we wanted to be partnered, if they hadn't split us up, I would be there right now." He pointed in the general direction of her spindle and shoved at the overfilled pack, trying to get it to close.

"Just wait until the next medic comes down." Obie rubbed at his face.

"That will take too damn long. I've done all I can, I just finished the last of the metal panels, the burgh is basically done. I'm not needed here. I'm needed there," he said.

"It could take months for you to get there, and you have no idea what kind of animals will be out there. You said it yourself, the big things have some kind of predator."

"Why are you trying to get me to stay here? You know I have to get to her." Troylus shook his head and slung the heavy pack onto his back.

"Fine, I do get that. But this could kill you." Obie sat on the tiny bunk with the mussed up blankets from Troylus's sleeplessness of the night before.

"Losing her would kill all the good parts of me, Obie. And, she's having our baby. I can't leave her alone with her injuries, and I really can't while she's pregnant. Their region won't be getting a spindle to bring more people down for longer than it will take me to walk there." He put a hand on Obie's shoulder who tensed up at the contact.

"You're a good friend," Troylus said, "I know you're trying to look out for me. But letting me go, and remaining my friend, *is* looking out for me."

Obie dropped his head and nodded.

"And you're a giant pain in the ass." Obie stood and Troylus's hand dropped from his shoulder as he laughed because he knew it was true.

"The real question is, how boring will this place be without me here to drag you past the edge of the burgh?"

Beyond the door of the bunk house where he had spent the last few nights, the sun was climbing through the sky and the sounds of the last of the burgh's buildings being put together rang through the air.

"We are the first spindle to get our burgh ready, did you know that?" Obie asked, walking along beside Troylus.

"How are we the first? Other people with abilities have to be assigned to the others too." Troylus shook his head, adjusting his pack where it was digging into the soft part of his shoulder where it met his neck.

"A few of them haven't started because they have more terraforming to do, but mostly it's seems we have the only untethered person with blue light that figured out he can use it to fix shit." Obie shrugged and Troylus cracked up laughing.

"You know, at some point you should really come see our

region." Troylus turned to Obie at the edge of the burgh and smiled, "I'm going to miss your way of looking at things."

Obie smiled and nodded, turned on his heel and walked back to where the rest of the crew was erecting some of the last homes.

Troylus waited while his friend walked out of sight and surveyed the burgh, the metal of the buildings shining in the oppressive sunlight just like the spindle would at their center when it returned from the Wheel.

Dark and light wood, harvested from some of the few trees they found in the area, large rocks, synthetic materials, and metal, so much metal, all of it together reminded him of the look of the inside of the ship.

But that made sense, no matter how much he didn't want the burgh he had helped build to be a reflection of the Chapter, it was. Of course it was.

He turned to make his way through the long grass for a while until he came to the dip in the mountain he had seen on the scans. It was the best way to get to her, the fastest way to get to her, but it would never be fast enough.

Picking up his pace, finding his rhythm in his steps, he reminded himself not to overdo it too much on his first day. He had a long way to go.

"Wait," Xander called from behind him and Troylus stopped.

"Did you hear something? Is she okay?" he yelled back across the field as Xander ran after him.

"No, I'm coming with you." Xander grimaced and adjusted the pack on his own back.

"You can't," Troylus said, shaking his head. There was no way he heard that right.

"I can. They don't need me here; they'll have another medic coming back with the spindle. The request was put in before it left." Xander was grinning, squinting into the too bright light of the day past Troylus's shoulder. He was probably the same age as Troylus or even a little older, but his face was still rounded and his dark skin was so smooth he looked much younger.

"But, Xander, it isn't like this is a quick and safe trip. It would be better for you, especially with leadership, if you stay here and travel between the regions on the spindles." Troylus tried to keep his voice level, to betray nothing of the seed of hope that was growing in him, that he might not be alone for the long journey and he might bring real medic help to Zellendine, and the even stronger fear that bringing Xander would slow him down and hurt Xander's chances for his future.

"Troylus, I know about your struggle with leadership, everyone does. I also know you're going off beyond the burgh on your own the first chance you get no matter what any of us say. Let me come and help Zellendine." Xander stared at him, his dark eyes intent and full of an iron will.

It was true that the likelihood every one of his crew members knew about his issues with leadership, even though he didn't talk about it, was high. And he wanted to bring the medic back to Zellendine, to help her if he couldn't.

He turned with his hands on his hips to look back toward the grass and the eventual pass through the mountains. The but, the list of reasons he should say no to Xander, the yeah that's great but, sat on his tongue as he bit his lip and tried to figure out if it was shittier to send him back to the burgh, or to take him with.

Finally, Troylus turned back to Xander and decided he didn't care which was shittier. The only thing he could afford to care about was Zellendine.

"Okay, but we are making this a damn quick trip," he said.

"Yeah, she needs us to get there fast." Xander shrugged and walked past him into the grass.

Troylus ran to catch up to him and ground his teeth together, this was not a good start.

"What I mean is, if you're going to slow me down, it would be better if you stay in this burgh and send a medic as soon as the spindles are running to her region."

Xander glanced at him and picked up the pace, setting his jaw and leaning a fraction further forward.

Good. Maybe this was going to work.

But the pack on his back was still digging into the spot between his neck and his shoulder, he was still tired after forcing his ability so hard since learning how bad she was, and the sweat was already starting to collect on his back as the heat of the day started in earnest.

15

ZELLENDINE

"AH," SHE CRIED, HER VOICE SMALL AND WEAK, HER THROAT parched and unable to form words.

Imogene appeared, her face inches above Zellendine's, her mouth open in a little o.

"Zellendine, you're awake."

But she wasn't awake, not really. She was in some halfway place.

She closed her eyes and grimaced while sparks of pain shot through her body like comets, trailing lasting agony.

No words came out of her mouth, just groans, low and hoarse. No words formed in her head, nothing that made sense, nothing beyond the overall impression of her shrunken world.

The world had become so small it consisted of only her nerve endings, their screams, and her growing desperation to go back to the dark.

"Hang on," Imogene said, dripping some water into her mouth. "Just hang on. Troylus is on the way. Hang on."

On the way, those words managed to pierce through the heavy veil in her mind. Those words and Troylus's name. He was on the way. But why wasn't he there with her already? And why wasn't she in the clinic with medics? Imogene wasn't a medic.

Zellendine strained against her own memory, pulled and tugged at it, trying to figure out how she knew Imogene was not a medic. She couldn't find it. She knew the other girl's name, but not how she met her, or what her assignment actually was. Looking for the answer was like looking into a black hole.

Above her loomed a strange dark fabric, past the edge of it was bright, garish light that made her vision blurry.

"Where?" she managed to say, her voice a rough sound more than a word.

"No spindle can get him here. I don't know where exactly he is right now." Imogene dripped more water into her mouth, her silver eyes in her dark face blurring together so she looked like silver was streaking all over her.

Spindle. Was Troylus on a spindle? Had he gone to the planet without her? How was he getting back to the ship without a spindle?

Her heart ached at his absence and the thought he had left her.

Moving, a small adjustment to try and escape the shooting pains, sent a wave of sharp knives through her arm and up her neck.

Plaintive wailing, she heard a mournful sound devoid of energy or will to outlast whatever was causing the person to sound that way. It made her want to go back to the dark. When she was in the dark she didn't have to hear suffering she couldn't help.

"Zellendine, shhh. Just don't move. I know it hurts, I'm trying, every day, I'm trying."

The crying stopped, each breath she took in and out was a

searing rasp that wrapped the cords of agony more tightly around her body.

"He's coming as fast he can."

Imogene's words turned back into unintelligible noise, something that Zellendine's mind would never be able to pick any meaning out of. But her eyes were closed, and the dark was creeping in at the edges, taking her back to the warm and better place in the black.

As it took her away from the girl who she couldn't remember clearly, the room she didn't recognize at all, and the circumstances she couldn't understand, the only thing Zellendine asked the universe was to allow her to stay asleep.

16

TROYLUS

The sky was darkening, they had to be getting close to the pass, and every bit closer to another night on the plain made the blood run hotter in his veins and his fists itch more to smash something.

"It should be just around the next bend," Xander said, more chipper than he had started out which made Troylus grind his teeth.

"You said that about the last rock," Troylus said, his voice almost betraying him.

"Well, any second, we'll see the dip. It's so clear on the holo, I'm sure we'll find it.

Troylus stomped faster, pulling ahead, not wanting to have the same pointless conversation again.

In the twilight of the plain, humming started and Troylus missed a step.

"Are they going to follow us the whole way?" Xander called from behind him, his voice uneven.

"Maybe. If the terrain works for them, they'll be good to have around."

Xander's footsteps pounded on the ground as he ran to catch up to Troylus.

"Why are you afraid of them? They're fine." Troylus shook his head looking at him.

"Because…" He looked back at Troylus for a second before returning his gaze to the long grass that hid the big beasts. "They have six eyes and they're huge."

"Six eyes? That's it?" It was everything Troylus could do not to laugh.

"Yes. I've never seen anything with six eyes except insects." He shivered and gripped the straps of his pack tighter.

"And that freaks you out?"

"Of course it does, it doesn't look natural. Besides, you've seen how damn big they are. If they wanted to kill us, all they would have to do was step on us." Xander turned to face forward, his pace picking up, and he swallowed so his Adam's apple bobbed.

Troylus couldn't suppress his smile. It wasn't because he was wrong, Xander had a point. He smiled because he could so easily see that more people would be scared of the animals, and he thought maybe that would mean they would be left alone.

After being accepted by them, he didn't want anyone to hurt them. Leaving them alone was the best option.

Rounding a corner, he saw it.

Cleaved into the rock, slicing right through the mountain itself, there was a deep dip. It would cut off days from their journey by saving them the need to climb up so far in elevation. To say nothing of the fact that he was sure some part of scaling the mountain in another place would have meant ascending near vertical rock faces.

"Good, we found it, now let's get up there a ways before we set up for the night," Xander said with a grin and hurried steps into the pass.

Troylus looked back out to the plain and nodded, hoping the animals would see him and know he appreciated their attempt to look after them. He turned back the way he had come, but he didn't see the burgh from that far away. Maybe in the light he would have been able to make out the shine from the sun on the metal.

But for that moment, if he hadn't known the burgh was there, if he hadn't helped build it, if he didn't know for a fact it was back there somewhere, he wouldn't have realized it.

Stepping into the pass, the rock took over for the grass in mere strides.

"Not much grows directly on this rock," Xander said from ahead of him as his steps grew louder and louder by crunching the rocks under his feet and he kicked at a little pile of small ones.

"No, but hopefully other regions have more vegetation," Troylus said, picking his way through an area full of small stones that looked less than perfectly steady.

"They better, if the only thing that will grow on the whole planet is grasses, how are we going to settle it long term?"

"Have you seen any of the reports from the other regions?"

"Only one I think. I wasn't paying that much attention to the terraforming reports, I'm not very good at making sense out of their numbers. Medic reports? No problem. But what the percentage of volcanic activity means in relation to actual circumstances on the ground? No idea," Xander said, looking back at Troylus and shrugging.

"Back on the ship I had a friend in the terraforming department," Troylus said, thinking of how differently he would have described Briar after everything that had happened. Friend was a very old description for him now. "So some of it was explained to me. It looks good as far as varied ecology from region to region if that helps."

"So, what you're saying is that there should be lots of different freaky animals and lots of plants," Xander said, with a laugh.

"Yeah." Troylus smiled, maybe it wouldn't be terrible to have Xander along now that they were in the pass and he knew for sure they were making progress.

"Just so you know, tomorrow is going suck, so don't get mad at me."

Troylus did laugh at that.

"How do you know tomorrow is going to suck?"

"Because, this terrain is already starting to hurt my legs."

"We just started, your legs are sore because we've been walking practically non-stop for two days." Troylus shook his head. "And why do you think I'm going to get mad at you?"

Xander stopped and looked back at him, one eyebrow high.

"Alright," Troylus said, laughing again. "Fine. I'll try not to get mad."

They walked on as the night crept ever closer, the gap in the rock growing darker faster than Troylus thought the plains would have.

Eventually they stopped and made their meager camp, Troylus unrolling a thick blanket and sighing that he had not been able to bring a pillow.

"Of all the things about this trek that are hard, why is it that I think not having a pillow is the worst?" Troylus asked, climbing into his blanket and taking a bar out of his pack.

"Because, you don't want to be angry and worried every minute of the day so you pour all your negative emotions into something innocuous that won't cost you long term like a missing pillow." Xander finished getting into his own roll, and taking a bite of his bar as he laid down.

Troylus's mouth dropped open and he stared at the lump that was Xander as he shewed on his bar with his eyes closed like he was going to fall asleep the second he was done and he hadn't just thrown a bomb into Troylus's well-being.

Zellendine needed him, she was right on the other side of the mountain, she was hurt and in pain, still in danger of not making it, and here he was complaining about a pillow because it was easier than being upset.

"I suck," he whispered, laying down himself and staring into the night sky as it turned to deep black and stars popped out of the dark.

There was no answer from Xander, no answer from the stars.

Finishing his bar, Troylus curled up on his side and apologized in his mind to Zellendine.

He had always hated apologizing, but damned if he wasn't used to it. He still didn't want to have to do it where most people were concerned, but he would beg forgiveness from her every day for the rest of their lives if she made it and that's what he had to do.

Somewhere in the back of his mind the fact that she was pregnant, that they might have a child together, was doing somersaults waiting for him to think about it. But if his own worry was too much for him to handle, dealing with the shock of her pregnancy was infinitely more than that.

Instead, he spoke to her in his mind, he told her he loved her, he begged her to get better, and then he went into the darkness of his sleep.

17

ZELLENDINE

Sometimes she was almost sure she knew where she was, it was right there, just beyond her grasp.

Zellendine reached for it, like she had scrambled to reach for the tank to slam it closed when the anomaly attacked the window. But unlike the last time she was desperate to grab onto something, this time she just couldn't get her grip.

Maybe she needed Troylus to remake the world again.

"But maybe I have to do it this time," she said, her voice still sounded broken, but it was the longest sentence she had been able to speak and Imogene's face appeared over her own again.

"Are you awake?" she asked, her eyes wide and her braids with the tail of the bright yellow tie around them hung down toward Zellendine's face.

"Yes," she said, although the y was lost in her choked pronunciation.

"Oh, Zellendine." She sighed and her smile was small and gentle. "Do you think you'll be able to eat something?"

Her stomach flopped about in her abdomen at the thought while the rest of her body cried out for the idea of food.

"I'm not sure," she said, and she had no idea how to explain.

"Be right back," Imogene said, and disappeared from overhead.

Zellendine's stomach growled, ending her argument with herself. No matter how much she was wasn't sure if she should try and eat, she had to.

She squinted at the dark thing blocking the light directly over her, was that a blanket? Why would a blanket be over her? Why didn't they just turn off the lights?

But no one was around to ask, the silence in the area directly around her was absolute.

Wait… no it wasn't.

A sound, multiple sounds, bounced around her, distorted and strange.

Her mind played through every part of the ship, trying to place her surroundings. But none of the places she knew would have had the same acoustics. Although maybe it was because of the crowding.

None of the explanations she came up with managed to explain her current reality.

And none of them came anywhere near explaining how she got hurt in the first place.

The medic part of her brain tried to take stock without knowing anything about her injuries.

Her shoulder, her arm, her neck, all on the left side of her body was a huge problem. Her head, something was seriously wrong with her head. The rest of her was probably minor injuries, she felt some irritating pain in her knees and on her hip on the same side as her problem arm. There were definitely lacerations and bone deep bruises on other parts of her.

But her self-assessment didn't explain the level to which she was still dizzy, or her inability to even shift in place without being hammered by her nerve endings as they screamed.

Footsteps squeaked along a hard heavy flooring surface and Imogene's face popped up in front of her.

"Okay, I got you some soup. The question is, do you want me to try and sit you up, or do you want me to spoon it into your mouth?"

"Spoon," Zellendine said, the thought of being sat up making her nauseous.

"And tell me what happened," she said, as Imogene cringed and sat back.

"Here," Imogene said, pouring a small bit of warm, thick soup into Zellendine's mouth which she swallowed greedily and her stomach growled at.

"Good." Imogene took a big breath and began to slowly feed her.

"What do you remember?"

"Troylus and I fought with Briar, and then we went to bed, the next day we were supposed to get on separate spindles, but Briar must have attacked me again, right?"

"No," Imogene said, her voice rough as she went back to feeding her. "You are on the planet. You've been here for months. We're still terraforming and at first we had trouble with comms."

Continuing to eat grew more difficult as Imogene spoke of a life Zellendine didn't know she had lived. Tears built in her eyes and her vision swam until they trickled out of the corners of her eyes and dripped down her temples to wet the edge of her hair.

"You were running up the stairs and tripped and fell head first into the metal grating before tumbling down an entire flight. You fractured your skull, broke your collar bone, and scraped yourself all over the place."

"Lacerations, skull fracture, collar bone, and..." Zellendine paused in listing her own injuries so she could swallow, not wanting to ask and knowing she had to. She had to know. "Brain damage?"

"Some."

Not moving, staring at the dark blanket waiting above her, she tried to imagine how long she had been in the dark, who was treating her, and her course of treatment.

"We have an extra medic?"

"They can't send anyone because we're still in the middle of the terraforming and we can't leave for the same reason. You are our only medic," Imogene said.

"How am I getting treatment? No one else can do it," she said, squeezing her eyes shut to stop the tears.

Imogene explained while she fed her more soup and gave her some water.

"So, what is the updated prognosis after using your ability? When will I be able to jump up and get back to working on things?" she asked, trying to smile and mostly just getting an uneven face twitch.

"The medic from the ship told me not to continue. He said that I did what I needed to stabilize you, to heal your brain, but the rest would have to get better on its own."

Her face came back into view, hanging not far above Zellendine's own, and she was grateful, but… it didn't make sense.

"I want you to know, I am very thankful you helped me, but why would you stop? There are no negative side effects. I saw Troylus heal someone."

"Zellendine," Imogene said, biting her lip.

"What?" Her voice was hushed, her throat felt much better and she could have asked the question more clearly and more forcefully, but her brain was setting off all the alarms within her. Imogene was hiding something.

Something was very wrong.

Unless the ship wanted her to suffer for her crimes against

the Chapter, but all of that had been forgiven. Or, at least she thought it had.

"Come on, Imogene, I need to know."

"Running scans, we found out that…" Imogene looked toward Zellendine's feet for a second before she returned her eyes back to stare into Zellendine's. "You're pregnant."

Zellendine smiled and tried to laugh, but it ended in a wheeze and a shot of pain.

"Very funny, Imogene. Tell me really, what's wrong with me that you had to stop?"

"I'm not trying to be funny. You're the first pregnant person on the planet."

She sucked in a breath that ended in a cringe and searing pain from her collar bone.

"That's not possible."

"But it's true."

And while it shouldn't have been possible, while it should have taken months for anyone on the planet to be able to have children like it had the other times they had colonized, and she had to have gotten pregnant on the ship, she thought about the birds and Yanna.

"On the ship, in the orchard, the birds were building nests and hatching their own eggs. One of the women from our shift got pregnant, but it was a fluke. I thought it was the universe's way of helping her." Her voice was barely audible and Imogene leaned in to listen, her face a mask as she pulled away again without comment.

Not that there was much to comment on.

She was pregnant. She should have had an abortion so her body could heal, it was the most medically sound decision. She knew that.

But she didn't want to. She wanted to have the fetus inside her grow into her baby.

"Troylus, does he know?" she asked, breathless, while her heart hammered away in her chest.

"Yes. And he's on his way."

Zellendine closed her eyes, trying to imagine where he was, what he thought about her being pregnant. But while she knew he would be panicked, about her injuries if nothing else, she had no idea what he thought about children.

All she could do was send a wish to the universe, that he would get there soon, and that she and the fetus would be healthy enough for her to hold her baby once the baby was born.

But first, the dark moved in to claim her for more time lost to the waking world.

1 8

TROYLUS

His hand slipped, scraping along the rough edge of one of the rocks, leaving behind a smear of deep red blood.

"Shit," he muttered, wiping the cut hand on his side, sucking a breath in through his teeth with a hiss, before he gripped the rock again.

"You okay?" Xander asked from somewhere below him.

He couldn't see Xander down there, but his voice sounded like he was navigating the steep climb better than he was.

"I'm fine, there's some sharp rocks up here, watch out."

Climbing again, he could see the top of the crag they were trying to get beyond, but it didn't look much closer than it had when they started up the damn wall of rock.

"This pass was supposed to be the easy way through," he said, pulling with his arms until the muscles in his forearms and back wanted to cramp.

"Use your legs more, you're going to strain your arms," Xander said.

"Very funny, if I could get my feet into a position to shove off with them instead of just hanging on to a tiny edge with the toe of my shoe, I would." He knew how to climb this damn thing, it wasn't like it was the first sheer cliff face they had managed to make it up.

"Just looking out for you."

Sure.

Troylus shut his eyes and took a couple deep breaths, he wasn't supposed to take shit out on Xander, he needed to just make this work and focus on what was in front of him, not how fucking long it was taking.

He pulled away from the rock enough to look down and find a better placement for his foot, then the other.

Focusing back to the rocks above him, he found the one he was aiming for and used his legs, making the grab.

It took longer than he wanted to scale the face, but pulling himself up onto the plateau at the top, cold wind whipping his hair into his eyes the second he was over the edge, he laid sprawled out on the ground and staring into the blue of the sky.

Done. Another cliff done, another obstacle passed, one more day, one more step closer to Zellendine.

Troylus levered himself up off the ground and was just sitting when Xander popped up over the edge, taking a seat beside him.

Looking out over the plains they had come from, dots of herds of the big beasts were scattered among the grass. They were easy to spot from way up there.

"I can't see the burgh from here," Troylus said, not sure if he wanted to or whether he wished he had or not.

"Nope, the pass wall blocks it, but that view is still amazing." Xander turned to him, a grin breaking out on his face and his eyes wide. "We should see what the other side is like."

Troylus smiled too and turned with him to see a view that almost couldn't have been more different than what he was expecting.

"We know where all the trees went," he said.

"How are none of them over on the other side?" Xander asked, his voice low like he wasn't looking for an answer but was just thinking out loud.

It was a good thing Troylus didn't think he expected an answer, because all he could do was shake his head in response.

The side of the plains had few trees and what was there were tall, spindly things, most of which had white peeling bark. But the side of Zellendine's burgh only remained mostly rock for a little ways, then it turned into lush, thick, green.

He had a hard time even telling the lay of the land, a hard time knowing if the same indentation in the rock was going to continue on that other side because there were so many trees and they were so tall it looked like a continuous wave of green.

"Look," Xander said, pointing off to one side.

And there it was, a depression in the trees.

It was massive, flat, and seemed to be full of brown murky water. In the middle of the giant field of gunky looking dirt, sat only the top of a spindle, everything else was buried deep in the ground.

"They said they had a swamp they had to terraform, for some reason I didn't expect how extensive it would be," Troylus said and Xander nodded beside him.

"What I want to know is, how much water are we going to have to navigate through to get there?"

Xander and Troylus turned to each other, Troylus could only shrug.

"Does it matter how much?" he asked, afraid that it did, at least for his timeline to get to Zellendine.

"No, I guess not. We have to go through it no matter what, right?"

He nodded and pushed himself up to standing, taking off

down the rocky hillside, little pebbles being sent pinging off the rocks around them, while Xander followed behind.

"At least this way isn't nearly as steep," Xander said from behind him and Troylus nodded.

No, it wasn't as steep, but he watched where he was placing his feet carefully anyway. The last thing he wanted was to fall on the way down and hurt himself somehow.

It didn't take long before they reached the edge of the trees, the first of them more spaced out than they were further down. The trees were deep, rich green with gnarled brown bark.

"Beautiful," he said, looking at the strange not leaves on the trees.

"Odd and beautiful," Xander said behind him.

He couldn't argue.

Moving deeper into the forest, the light from the sun high overhead was filtered through the thick branches, leaving them in a daytime twilight world of perpetual green sunset.

"When you were little did they read the stories to you?" Xander asked.

"You mean the ones we learned on or the stories of what the planet would be like?" In their endeavor to always look forward they were very limited in what stories they were allowed to read or to tell, but there were a few that were deemed okay only as children learned. Fantastical stories of creatures not human.

"The learning stories of the Fae. This looks like what I always pictured their world would be," Xander said.

Looking around at the dappled pattern of the light, the tinge of green and brown to it, and the almost sentinel quality of the trees themselves, Troylus had to agree.

"I'm glad Zellendine and I are settling on this side of the mountains," Troylus said, imagining leaving the burgh to live among the trees.

"And I'm glad I came with you. This is amazing," Xander

said, his head tilted back so he watch the boughs flutter in a breeze that didn't penetrate deep enough for them to feel it.

Somewhere deep in the woods, a haunting sound rent the air, it started low and grew as it went higher and higher. It didn't seem to end, and other voices joined it.

Troylus stopped walking and Xander froze in place next to him.

Eventually the sounds stopped, leaving them standing in the gloam, with little idea what it was, or what they were supposed to do about it.

"We know where the predators of the big beasts are," Troylus whispered as all the hairs on his arms stood on end.

19

ZELLENDINE

"No, use that wrap above the one you grabbed," she said, pointing one finger of the hand not strapped down to her body.

"This?" Maurice asked, holding up the right one finally.

She nodded and watched closely as he wrapped Corto's twisted ankle, ready to correct any mistake.

But he succeeded. They were all getting better at patching up each other's wounds while she tried to heal her own with nothing more than time and her beat up body and brain.

"Well done, Maurice. And Corto," she said, narrowing her eyes at him. "This is the second time you've managed to need a medic *today*."

"I know, Zellendine. Sorry, I'll be careful." He kissed his own hand and touched it to the top of her head before he limped away.

"People keep doing that," she said, the plush confines of the makeshift medical chair that propped her up to a sitting position kept her from shaking her head.

"Everyone thinks that they're giving you a blessing to heal," Maurice said, putting the rest of the supplies away.

"How do they figure that?" And how did they go from the reticence to touch at all after a lifetime of the protocols to this?

"Because, we all want to be able to help. And Imogene had to put her hands on your head to use her ability, we had to touch you to pick you up, and you've had to give each of us medic care at some point." He shrugged and kissed his hand, making a slow study of the act of reaching out and giving the top of her head the lightest touch.

Zellendine couldn't move her makeshift chair by herself, so after he left her, the only thing in her field of vision was the medic bay. That was alright, she wasn't sure yet what to make of what Maurice had told her.

"You know," Imogene said, surprising her by popping up behind her and turning her chair so she could see the rest of the spindle's main space. "What took the Chapter years to bury deep in our heads, you, by just living, have undone in months."

"More like weeks. Not many random touches happening around here before I got hurt."

"No, but the seeds for the change all came from you, running around with all that stuff, treating all our small scrapes and bruises while the rest of us watched."

Imogene bent to look at Zellendine's feet, to check and see if she needed to attach the machines that made sure her leg circulation remained good.

"That will make leadership happy," she said, sarcasm heavy in her voice.

"Who cares if leadership is happy about it?" Imogene made eye contact with her and Zellendine's heart thumped.

"Be careful," she whispered, suppressing the shudders that wanted to run through her and would hurt all her sore muscles in the process.

"Zellendine, it's different now."

Imogene walked off to the service and started to putter

around. It must have been near time for the midday meal, but Zellendine wasn't hungry. She was too confused to be hungry.

Leadership... Something was tickling her brain that she needed to do about leadership, something was in there, in the pieces of her mind that didn't want to be looked at, that would make leadership even more unhappy than the complete abandonment of the protocol.

But what was it?

She stared out at the cavernous main room, taking in the scope of the ceiling, it was so high she didn't understand why there weren't five more floors. What was the point in it being so soaring when the spindle was only a transport vehicle? And why were the lights always on?

It didn't make sense, but so much about the Chapter didn't make sense to her.

The makeshift walls that everyone had built to give themselves their own rooms were the only things that made the space not just a huge echo chamber devoid of personality and as cold to look at as it was to the touch.

Right next to her blanket and crate collection that was actually her room, there were pipes with panels between them of... something that Zellendine couldn't place.

"You ready for some food?" Imogene asked, coming to her side with Corto.

"Sure, but is that your room next to mine?" she asked Imogene.

"Of course, I needed to be right with you all the time at first."

Corto pushed her chair with Imogene over to the service area.

"What are your panels made out of?" Zellendine wanted to look at them closer, they almost looked like metal, but they weren't silver, grey, or black. Instead they were a warm brownish orange color and a blue tinged green. She had never seen anything like it.

"It's some kind of metal that we found while making the tunnels. I flattened it and used it because I thought it was pretty."

"Tunnels? I mean, yeah, it is pretty, but what tunnels?"

"Oh, we should show her before we all eat." Corto pushed on her chair so it pivoted to the side, but Imogene pushed back and the chair just stopped in the middle of the room.

"What? Why not?"

"Because, I don't know if the tunnels are totally safe," Imogene said, her voice like she was trying not to yell at him.

"Imogene, I would like to see them. I don't get why this is such a big deal." She wanted to be able to get out of her damn chair and walk her happy ass over to see whatever she wanted.

"Fine. Go ahead with Corto, have someone else help you though because I won't do it."

"Seriously?" she asked as Imogene's voice faded with the sound of her stomping footsteps. "What was that about?" Zellendine asked Corto.

"I have no idea, but I'll ask Maurice. Hang on."

The sound of his retreating footsteps, uneven with his limp made her feel every bit of the healing she had yet to do.

Her stomach was growing, and in the process it seemed recovery for her own injuries were delayed.

But she had to get walking again. She had to find a way to get moving.

Planting her good hand on the arm of her makeshift chair she shifted her feet so they were flat on the cold of the floor. The pressure on her skin, muscles, nerve endings, and bones felt like too much at first. Even just resting there, not taking her weight on them.

Trying to stand was more difficult.

Her collar bone was in agony as she moved, and her head throbbed more with every beat of her heart the further she got it from the floor.

"No. Have you lost your fucking tether," Imogene yelled, popping up in front of Zellendine's face.

"Yes," Zellendine said and Imogene blinked before she bit her lip and nodded.

"Okay, fine, you win. Sit down before you fall down, and I'll take you to a tunnel."

Imogene helped her get comfortable and supported again, but Zellendine knew she needed to do the same thing the next day, and the day after. She had to start building up her strength, not just heal her wounds.

"Let's go see the tunnels really quick, but we aren't staying out there very long."

"Why do you have such a problem with me going out there when you don't seem upset about anyone else seeing them?" Zellendine asked, her voice quiet as Imogene pushed her chair all by herself.

Behind her, Imogene sighed.

"They remind me of the hallways on the ship."

Her voice was quiet and soul wrenchingly sad.

"I don't understand; how does that matter?" Zellendine didn't want to ask, she didn't want to make it worse for her friend, but she needed to ask so she would understand how not to make it worse.

"Someone I… know, lost her partner in the accident and she almost died but was blown to the other side of the door and she didn't know how." Her voice went from tripping over the word know to devoid of emotion.

But Zellendine could picture it.

"You saw the woman you love about to die with her partner

and your ability snapped into action." Zellendine said, the sound of a choked down sob from behind her was the only answer.

"Don't worry, Imogene, I can go see the tunnels later. You don't have to take me."

The chair stopped and it shifted like she was leaning on the back of it.

"Thank you."

"Let's get something to eat."

"Absolutely."

But after her chair was turned and they were heading to the service, Zellendine thought of one more things she needed to know.

"Does she know? The woman you love?"

"No."

"Tell her, before she gets assigned to another region. Tell her."

Imogene didn't answer, but Zellendine smiled. Her friend deserved so much love, and maybe it would help to heal the woman's broken heart over her lost partner.

But her mind stopped short and Zellendine's smile faltered as she thought about what she had put Troylus through because of a misstep.

Getting better was all that could matter to her, getting better and being healthy enough to have their baby and see Troylus again.

2 0

TROYLUS

"This sucks," Xander said through chattering teeth, wrapping his arms tighter around his body and ducking under a sodden, low hanging branch. "Man, I hope she will appreciate how much you're going through."

"Shut up," Troylus said with a laugh and shake of his head as he stepped around another rivulet of water snaking through the forest floor. "One day, you'll find someone who makes it worth it for you to do a lot more than walk through the rain."

"Not me, I have no interest," Xander said, shivering and ducking his head further into his uniform.

"Like none now, or none ever. Because you've been stuck next to me for weeks and I don't think I would be interested if I was stuck with me either."

Xander laughed, laughed so hard he didn't watch where he was going and stepped, with a splash, into a puddle.

"Fuck." He looked at Troylus and shook his head, while his grin didn't slip and Troylus crinkled his nose in sympathy.

"It isn't because I'm stuck with you, although if I ever was going to get involved with someone romantically, you're not my type."

Troylus had his turn to laugh.

"Fair," he said, still laughing.

Under the heavy canopy of the trees, the already reduced light further greyed by the cloud cover and rain, deepened perceptibly.

"Shit, is it getting dark already?" Xander asked.

Troylus squinted up into the branches, his face pelted by the heavy drops of rain.

"Looks like it." Troylus looked around them, scanning the area for any possible place for them to spend the night off the sodden ground.

"One of us should climb a tree again and see how close we are to the spindle. Maybe we should use the glasses and keep walking." Xander shook his shoulders like he was trying to keep warm.

"You head up the tree, the climb will get your blood moving faster. Here, I'll give you a boost," Troylus said, bracing himself next to a large tree with branches low enough that Xander could climb it. He linked his hands together and held them out for the soaked shoe that Xander placed there, shoving him up the second he got braced with his hands and jumped off the ground with his other foot.

Xander scrambled, from one branch to another, up the tall tree.

Ducking his head, Troylus squeezed closer to the trunk. The driest place he had been all day was close to the base of the tree, and even there, giant drops collected along the tree itself fell on his head.

Miserable, the weather was miserable when he had no idea how long it would be before he was inside somewhere, warm and dry.

"Troylus," Xander called, his voice almost drowned out by the steady downpour.

"What? You okay?" he yelled back, tilting his head back and cupping his hands around his mouth, hoping he could be heard.

"Come up here."

He stared into the dripping bits of sky he was able to see through the green above him and blinked.

Why would he need to climb the tree too?

But he didn't want to scream back and forth arguing about it. They would both only end up with hurt voices, and he might wind up climbing the damn tree anyway.

On his way up, every step and hand on a soggy branch made his grip tighter and his steps firmer. No way was he going to fall and kill himself because of some rain. Not when he already scaled a mountain.

Finally, he spotted Xander's feet on a branch above him. He moved to the other side of the trunk so he wasn't putting his weight in the same place.

The last section of the tree was thick with the deep green boughs that weren't leaves. But even though they were different from leaves, they still held plenty of rain that soaked him through to the skin as he shoved his head and shoulders through the net they formed and into the downpour on the other side.

Rain lashed against his face, plastered his hair to his head, and dripped down his back inside his uniform.

It was so loud and the wind so cold he ducked back down, closer to the boughs after only a second of being so exposed to the elements.

"Why the fuck am I up here?" he yelled, his voice yanked from him to be thrown away on the wind.

Xander didn't answer from where he was crouching close to the top of the tree, he lifted a hand and pointed behind Troylus.

He turned around to see what was behind him and froze.

They were not close enough to the spindle to walk all night and get there the next day. But that wasn't what made Troylus unable to move as he was whipped by rain and wind.

Overhead, the sky was a steel grey with spikes of angry lightning flashing through it, and above the small piece of the spindle they could still see, purple balls of energy shot through the clouds to attack the spindle, again, and again. The cold of the outside was nothing to the ice that flowed through him.

"I have to get there. It's trying to hit Zellendine," he said, paying no attention to where he placed his hands and feet as he made a mad dash to get down. He didn't know how he knew in his bones that it was there for her, but he did. The exact same thing he felt when he watched the anomaly attack, was running through him.

"Stop, Troylus," Xander yelled above the sound of snaps of the small twigs they both encountered as they went.

"No, she needs me. It won't get her if I'm there," he yelled, not bothering to slow his descent.

"Troylus, you can't get killed in the process. It's too far."

"I missed it. I fucking missed it. It was in the storm and the color in the sky. I should have seen it."

His foot slipped and left him dangling by his hands, slick with the rain.

"Shit, don't move," Xander yelled, speeding up his own way down.

Troylus found another branch with a knee and swung his feet up to it as carefully as he could as the bark dug into his palms.

"Don't do that shit again," Xander said, leaning his forehead against the trunk as Troylus stood up on the branch and hugged his chest against the bark while he sucked down breath after breath.

"How do I just sit here?" Troylus yelled, not taking another step as shivers ran through his body.

"You do it knowing that if you die on the way you can't do shit to protect her and you'll never see your kid." Xander was no longer yelling but his voice carried to Troylus anyway.

He banged his forehead against the trunk, squeezing his eyes shut and grinding his teeth.

"This is killing me. I have to get to her. I need to be there."

"I know, Troylus. But you can't be right this second. You have to trust the people with her to look out for her."

It didn't matter that he knew Xander was right. It didn't matter that he knew running through the woods in the middle of the night with less than perfect night glasses on, to a destination he still couldn't reach for days, was not an option.

Everything in him wanted to get there, at that second.

Part of him didn't care about the risk or the realities, but the rest of him wrestled that part into submission.

"We wake early," he said, finding a place where two branches met that he could sit on for the night.

Xander didn't answer, just moving through the tree to find his own place.

Troylus was no longer cold, his heart raced and his body was so hot it felt like he had been running.

But he couldn't run, he had to sit.

Sit and wait.

Wait for the day he finally made it to her. For the time he could be there, they could send the message, cut ties with the Chapter, and make their life in the peace of somewhere he could create for her that no purple attack would ever find her again.

He couldn't imagine where that place would be if the thing in space could come to the planet, but there had to be one. And he was going to find it.

2 1

ZELLENDINE

"Okay, one more step," Imogene said, holding her hands out on either side of Zellendine's arms.

Zellendine had to focus on the act of lifting her left foot, the toe wanting to drag until she pulled on the muscles in her shin to lift it enough to clear the ground.

Finally, it worked, and she was able to move it a few inches forward before she set her foot down again. The second it was firm, flat on the floor, Imogene caught her arms and Corto scooted her chair in behind her so she could be lowered into it.

Zellendine leaned back and closed her eyes, taking deep breaths, her heart racing. Sweat collected in the small of her back and around her growing belly.

"That sucked," she said, her voice an exhausted wheeze.

"You made it fifteen steps today. I'm so proud of you," Imogene said.

"Fifteen steps and I feel like I've been running for hours. It makes no sense." She started to shake her head and stopped herself, her collar bone should have been mostly healed, but it still hurt too much to move her neck around.

"Zellendine, you know why it makes perfect sense," Corto said, laughing as he helped push her chair to the service where the midday meal was about to start.

She did know why, she had overseen others going through physical therapy after injuries, and she knew she wasn't just retraining her muscles how to move in a way that was efficient and actually worked, but she was creating whole new neural pathways around the areas damaged in her fall that Imogene had not been able to heal. But knowing something intellectually and understanding something from the inside were two different things.

Part of her wondered if, even if Imogene continued her ministrations, her brain injury would still be the kind that meant something was lost that couldn't be recovered, only worked around anew. But she would never have the answers to all their questions. Even after all that had happened, what they knew of the abilities was limited.

The sounds of the others moving around in the service, getting the food ready at the table was a kind of music, the song of her friends.

She opened her eyes and watched as they did what they needed to and she sat in her chair doing what she needed to do.

Her eyelids felt heavy and her blinks grew longer as her body relaxed after her steps.

"Are all of you going to move into the burgh houses?" she asked, trying to stay awake.

"Where else would we live?" Maurice asked over his shoulder.

"In here. In the spindle."

Maurice laughed and a few others joined in.

"So that's a no," she said, looking at the table in front of her and biting her lip. Apparently they thought she had lost her tether a long time ago and was way out in space, but if she was able to go outside whenever she wanted via the tunnels, and she was planning on staying near the Chapter, she would have made a home inside the big space that had become one for her in the time she had been in it.

"This place is too big, and I bet it would feel even more massive if it was just a family living in here." Imogene sat down next to her and handed her a damp towel.

She nodded and used her good hand to wipe her face, neck, and both forearms.

"After everyone goes to bed tonight, I was wondering if I could go to the wet room and take a bath," she whispered to Imogene while the others working in the service talked about where in the burgh they were hoping to have a house one day.

"Of course," Imogene said, her eyebrows high.

Having Imogene brush out her hair and hand her damp towels to wipe down with was great, but she was pretty sure she was stinky by then. The only time she had spent in the wet room was to do her business and that was not great when she had to be picked up and put back in her chair until just recently.

"Are you really going to run into the woods with Troylus and never let us see this kid?" Maurice asked, bringing the food to the table with the others.

"No, we'll still need to come to the burgh to trade. Besides, any of you are welcome to visit us out in those woods whenever you feel like it," she said, smiling at the shocked look on his face.

"Leave the burgh?" His mouth hung open and his eyes were wide.

"For just a little while to visit, but you don't have to."

She knew it wasn't a popular decision among her crew mates, but she had no idea they were actually afraid of what she was planning to do until that moment.

"We don't even know what animals are out there yet. Maybe you should stay in the burgh for a while and then move." Corto said, taking a bite.

In the back of her mind there was the feeling she had forgotten something again. There was a reason beyond just wanting to be away from the Chapter that made their plan to live outside the burgh important. But why that was a fact, which she *knew* it was, floated just beyond her grasp.

"Troylus and I have a plan." It was all she could say to make sense of her decision, and it seemed flimsy, even to her. But any other explanation was lost to her injury.

"At least you're together in your plan, even though I think it isn't the best option in the universe." Maurice shook his head as he took another helping.

She did the best she could with her good hand, but by the time everyone else was done she had only managed to eat half her meal.

They talked a lot and said nothing while she ate until she was full, it was becoming a habit of theirs. The conversations were always about things that didn't matter, and they mattered more to her than she was able to say.

When she finished, she sat back in her chair and joined in the conversation about the best way to block the light in their rooms so they could sleep. Her body was past the effort of taking her precious few steps, but every word out of someone's mouth made her eyes heavier and her muscles more sore.

"Are you going to fall asleep on us again, Zellendine?" Corto asked, a gentle smile on his face.

"No, it just takes a lot out of me."

"How about we take you to check out the tunnels now, I bet that would wake you right up," he said.

"I don't think that's a good idea," Imogene said, freezing in place with a plate in her hand she was collecting to clean up.

"We'll only take a quick look at the cascade." Corto popped up from the table and tapped Maurice as he got behind her chair.

Maurice joined Corto in maneuvering her away from the table and toward the doorway to the tunnel.

Imogene stayed in the same position, standing next to the table, with a plate in her hands while she chewed on her top lip and stared after them.

"What is the cascade?" Zellendine asked, trying to shake off the look on Imogene's face.

"A beautiful side effect of terraforming," Corto said.

"I still don't know what that means." A million possibilities ran through her mind to explain what he said, but none of it fit with the word cascade and she decided she suffered from a lack of imagination.

"You just have to see it; I don't even know how I would begin to explain it." Maurice sounded like a little kid who just saw their first comet.

"This thing is that exciting?" she asked, trying not to laugh because it was so cute, she didn't want to discourage him.

"Just wait," Corto said.

She smiled and wondered at the jagged edges of the doorway as they passed into the tunnel. The opening was large, her room could fit inside it twice, and it seemed like a strange choice, but the tunnel on the other side was about the same size.

The edges of the opening may have been jagged, rough cut metal, but the tunnel on the other side was dirt smoothed and hardened to the same finish as the metal inside the spindle.

Of all the things she knew about the terraforming process from Briar, she had never heard much about this strange feat she was moving through.

It ran in both directions from the door, but Corto and Maurice both turned left without saying a word to each other.

She didn't know what the cascade was, but they sure did and it seemed the tunnel only led to it on one side.

She sat up straighter and tried to see as far ahead as she could, but the light in the tunnel was poor.

Light poured in from the too bright main cavern and someone had attached a light near the doorway on the tunnel side of the opening, but there was no other illumination. So the further they got away from the doorway, the more the light waned, it didn't help that there was a slight curve to the tunnel itself and soon they would find themselves beyond the point where the light would reach.

"Wait," she said, a dull, constant thrum was growing in volume, "What is that?"

Corto and Maurice didn't answer, but Maurice patted her shoulder as they pushed her along.

Every step they took, the noise grew louder.

Until the curving edge of the tunnel revealed a wall of falling water, the noise of it an overwhelming and awesome roar.

Maurice and Corto stopped and came to stand on either side of where she sat, with her mouth open and her mind blank.

She never thought she would see something so incredible be an accident of terraforming.

"Happy accident," she said, her voice pulled away into nothing. Even she didn't hear it, it was drowned out completely by the cascade before her.

The air in this section of the tunnel was strangely chilled, and she shivered, sending a wave of exhausted pain through her muscles.

She needed to get back and lay down, but she promised herself to come back often. It was just too beautiful.

Zellendine tapped Maurice on the arm with her good hand and he signaled to Corto it was time to go.

As they turned her around a hissing boom of purple light slammed into the wall of water, sending spray flying through the tunnel to soak them.

2 2

TROYLUS

"I'M NOT SURE I'VE EVER BEEN THIS COLD," XANDER SAID, shivering with his arms wrapped tight around him and his teeth chattering.

"The rain has to stop sometime. Maybe we should wrap ourselves in our blankets." Troylus swiped his dripping hair out of his eyes, but there was no getting away from the wet dripping down his back and soaking through every bit of his sodden uniform.

"Would they get wet too? I think we should save them for nightfall." A large shiver shook Xander so hard he gritted his teeth together, but to his credit he didn't stop walking.

"Nightfall is really going to be cold." Troylus didn't want to agree, he wanted another layer of warmth, but Xander was right.

He shoved a branch out of the way, waiting to release it until Xander had cleared it too. When he did release it, it snapped back sending the rain coating it flying.

"Is it just me, or are the trees thicker here?" Xander asked, stepping around another branch in their way.

"They're thicker. By a lot, it's been getting worse slowly since we came down the mountain," Troylus said, studying the trees directly in front of them for whether he thought he could use his ability to smash through a bunch of them.

"Are we sure we're still going the right direction? Should we climb?" Xander squinted up into the canopy above them and Troylus sighed.

"Probably, but fuck this is too damn slow." He rubbed his face, slick with rain and heating up with anger.

"Don't worry, we should be almost there by now." Xander smiled and grabbed a hold of one of the nearby branches, starting to climb.

The forest around them was loud with the noises of the ongoing storm and the activity of whatever small creatures lived there that made a steady background noise of small chatter.

But as Troylus stood as close to the trunk as possible, some of the volume around him went down.

He looked to the spots of sky he could see through the boughs, half expecting to for there to be purple balls of power shooting at him.

Above him though was just the regular storm, nothing that would have given him a second thought, except the sounds of the forest grew quieter still. It didn't make sense.

Straining his ears, he tried to pick up on anything that would have explained it.

For some reason he couldn't explain, it unnerved him that the forest was falling silent. It didn't stop the sound of the storm, but it was too quiet otherwise and every drop, every clap of thunder, seemed louder to his ears.

Xander making his way down the tree grew even louder than the storm, the boughs snapping and the limbs creaking with his descent.

Jumping off the last of the branches, he landed next to Troylus and rubbed his palms against the thighs of his uniform before wrapping his arms around himself again.

"We're on the right path," he said.

And a scream, harsh, guttural, and piercing ripped through the air followed by a wailing howl.

"Fuck," Troylus said, grabbing Xander and pulling him to his side against the tree trunk.

It sounded like the things making the sounds were right on top of them.

"What was that?" Xander whispered.

"Shhh." Troylus didn't want to explain, and he wasn't even sure if he needed to. Xander probably knew the answer to his question, but he didn't want to face it either, and he assumed that was why he asked the question.

Crashes, the sounds of snarling and snapping, seemed to come from everywhere at once.

He scanned the trees around them, trying to find the actual location of whatever was happening, but the trunks were too thick, the spaces between them too small for him to even narrow it down.

And every time a branch bounced after dropping a long collected amount of water, it made him jump.

Through the trees to their right, just showing around the edge of the trunk before the sight line was cut off by branches, he saw a flash a white followed by another flash of shining grey.

Nudging Xander with an elbow and staring at the small window of space, he raised a hand and pointed.

Xander leaned over so he was able to see along his arm, and leaned forward, closer to whatever was going to cause the vicious assault of sounds to continue to rend the air.

Shoved back by Xander's whole body slamming into him

and dragging him to a branch, Troylus lost his ability to breath. His breath was knocked out of him, he was left gasping for air as Xander scaled the tree again.

A split second later, he still tried to inflate his lungs as the little space they had just been exploded in fur and snapping jaws.

Troylus crouched down on the other side of the branch, not trusting his own ability to breathe or the safety of making a move upward while the white, muscular, four legged animal with the short, thick fur and small rounded ears snarled and shrieked, its mouth gaping open and exposing two rows of pointed teeth with two of them so long they hung past its bottom jaw when it was shut.

It fought three silver grey, long haired four legged creatures only a fraction smaller than it was. They were not so fearsomely equipped in teeth or claw, but they made up for it in their seemingly coordinated attacks of fetes and quick thrusts.

All of the animals had three eyes facing forward in their heads.

Predators.

Now he more than understood the beasts of the plains being so huge.

They had to be just to survive.

What chance did that leave him?

He was able to breathe again, but he slowly took air in and let it out, wanting to move as little as possible until their fight was over and they moved on.

But why were they fighting among themselves? What set them off? Weren't they just supposed to have different territories? He knew so little of fauna of any planet, but he could have sworn that was the story he was told as a child.

In front of him, the pointy ears of one of the smaller, grey animals twitched in his direction. It turned and looked at him, growling and showing its teeth.

The big white creature took the chance to swipe it with a massive paw and long, sharp looking claws that sunk into the side of the other before it sent it tumbling through the air to slam against a tree. The injured animal yelped, and its comrades went to its side, snarling until it stood and they left under the baleful eyes of the white creature.

Of the two options, if he was going to be left near one of them, he wasn't sure the white one gave him the best chance at survival.

As the last of the smaller ones limped through the trees, the white creature with the oversized teeth screamed the same bone chilling scream they had heard before.

He couldn't afford to lift his head and check to see where in the tree Xander was.

Xander could have been in an even worse position than he was for all he knew.

Maybe the thing could climb.

Its ears twitched, it's long, tree limb like tail swished in a motion that was equal parts fluid and abrupt, like a languid thing that snapped on either end of the swing.

Lowering its head, the shoulders of its front legs rolled as it turned and looked directly at him with all three of its eyes.

No matter the water pasting his hair to his head, he felt every single follicle ripple and raise under its glare.

Don't do it. Not yet.

His ability might not work against the animal, but there was no way it would save him if he used it too early and the damn thing got around whatever he managed to do.

But his fingers twitched, and his ability built up within him, threatening to spill out before he wanted it to just because of his own feelings.

The animal didn't bend its knees, it didn't crouch, it hardly moved, but somehow Troylus knew when it was going to make its leap to attack.

One second it was on the ground, and the next it was leaping through the air, its mouth open and snarling.

He raised his hands and screamed, blue light exploding out of him to slam a tree from nearby into the animal and stack itself like he was going to use it to build a house in the middle of the forest.

Shrieks of the creature rent the air while it rubbed at its own face with a paw.

It looked at him, its lip curling back over teeth big enough to pierce through him.

All he could do was swallow down the urge to run and lift his hands, preparing to use his ability until it ran out.

Troylus hoped it would outlast the white fur covered death before him.

Below the sounds of the storm, the thrumming of his own heart, and his heavy, rough breaths, his ears picked up on a deep, low hum that oscillated at a pace faster than his heart pounded.

The hairy beasts, leading with their horns, barreled through the trees, taking some of them with them.

Uprooted trees slammed into the white predator, sending it reeling back and fleeing through the woods.

He couldn't do anything except cower next to the trunk, back up to a limb, cover his head with his arms, and close his eyes while the cacophony of the crashing and destruction of the forest happened right in front of him.

Were they trying to help? Or were they just attacking the predator to protect themselves?

There were no easy answers, and as the noise settled down, the only thing left the creaking and cracking of downed trees being further trampled by creatures bigger than the predators, he opened his eyes.

Directly in front of his face were another set of eyes.

23

ZELLENDINE

Fast on the heels of the first blast another one slammed into the water, shards of it managed to make their way through.

One lodged in her chair right next to her leg, another slammed into her still not fully healed collar bone. The pain was enough to rip a scream from her lungs and force her body to contort in ways that only hurt her further.

Maurice and Corto shoved at her chair, all of them hurtling down the tunnel faster than the chair had ever moved before.

She was dripping wet and writhing, trying to focus all her effort on not hurting herself more, and failing.

They made it back to the doorway of the main area and Corto leaned against the back of the chair, Maurice laid down on the floor. All of them heaved in gulps of breath.

In the service, Imogene spotted them and called out to the whole crew, gathering everyone together and running to their sides.

Purple pieces of light with sharp, strange weight to it flaked off of her and fell into her lap.

Someone brushed the remaining shards aside with a towel while she screamed through clenched teeth.

When she ran out of breath and they stepped back from her she realized someone was crying.

Twisting to see what was going on, sharp stabs radiated through her body and spots appeared in her vision.

But when it cleared, she saw that Maurice had a shard hit his abdomen and blood poured from the wound while Imogene leaned over him and light poured from her, wrapping and swirling around him.

"No," she cried, her voice weak and plaintive.

She started barking orders and dropped to the floor beside him, the impact jarring her collar bone and making the dots reappear in her vision.

But she ground her teeth and stuck her hand right into the swirls if light.

Maurice was still alive, that much was at least clear, but he wasn't doing well, and she could only guess at how long he would last.

She issued more orders in a voice that sounded tortured, trusting they would get the right supplies. The second they appeared next to her she went to work with her one good hand.

Until the last thing she had to do required two.

Gritting her teeth, with a snarl and a guttural scream, she brought her bad hand up and went to work. Using both made sweat drip down her face. It got in her eyes and joined with the water that already covering her.

Imogene ran out of power and slumped to the side, caught by Corto and the others.

"Put her in her room, she'll sleep it off and be fine," she said, her voice was hard and steady, as were her hands as she continued to work on Maurice.

Finally, she finished and went still, unable to move any further, unable to get up or even back away.

But there was one more thing to do.

Someone handed her a holo and she rested it on her injured hand while she tapped with the other, going right to the scans she needed and checking everything about Maurice.

Whatever ability Imogene had, or maybe it was her own medic care for him, he was going to recover and live, but it had been a narrow thing.

One last scan told her what she needed to know for her own peace of mind. If they hadn't worked together, he wouldn't have made it.

The brave idiot, laid out in front of her, his uniform torn open to expose the new lines that would form into scars from where she had patched him back together on the outside, had managed to run her through the tunnel while he was bleeding and toxins were flooding his body from a perforated intestine and pierced liver.

Her collar bone, its knot of thickened and freshly healed bone, had stopped the shard that would have gone all the way through her shoulder. If it had hit her in the chest… She would have died before they even got back to the main room.

"Imogene," she said, her voice starting to give out so it sounded hoarse and scratchy, "she should know when she wakes up that he'll live, and it was likely only because of her."

None of them needed to know the details, not even Maurice. They didn't need to know that she had sewed him up because Imogene's ability was even weaker now than it was just months before when she had to heal Zellendine.

But she knew, she knew that her efforts helped, and Imogene's exhaustion ensured he wouldn't die of sepsis.

Her hands dropped the holo, which fell into her lap along

with her bad hand, the other she let drop all the way to the ground next to her.

"Can someone get me the arm brace I used to wear?" she asked, blinking long and slow, no longer caring that her voice was so bad it might not ever recover, although she did wonder how long she screamed in the noise of the tunnel when no one but the water could hear her.

The brace appeared before her and hands of her crew helped her put it on, only causing her vision to blur and blacken at the edges a few times.

On the ship, she would get surgery, removal of the pieces too small to heal, plates and screws, and maybe a graft to repair the shattered bone.

Instead, she was relying on the brace to hold it steady, and the chair to keep all the shards in a pocket of inflammation and immune response, in the hopes it didn't pierce an artery and cause her to bleed out internally.

Her arm and hand might not ever allow her to do the same level of activity with it as she had before, but if it healed enough for her to stay alive, maybe she could hug her baby with it when they were born.

Getting back into the chair was an act of will, her legs wobbled, her knees ached, even the thought of sitting back down, the jarring it would cause on her injury, was enough to make her simply want to fall over.

But Zellendine did get back in the chair, she even kept her energy up enough to drink a glass of water when it was offered and ask for no one to remove her from her chair while she slept.

The second the water was done, her eyes closed and she lost the ability to open them again.

Someone placed a blanket over her after someone else removed the shard from her chair.

Maybe they thought she might hurt herself on it, but she

wasn't going to move for a while. They probably didn't know that, but she did. Oh, she did.

Nothing in the universe could make her get up and move for a while.

Yet sleep eluded her.

Instead, she ran the purple light attack through her mind, again, and again.

A thing from space, the anomaly turned purple attack object, had managed to follow her to the ground.

Would she ever be safe from it?

The only place she was sure she remained safe from it was in the spindle proper. Somehow it had protected her for so long she forgot that something she couldn't name and didn't understand at all, hated her and wanted her dead.

Part of her understood Briar's anger, even part of her understood the anger of all the people changed against their will. Maybe not that they all seemed to hate her specifically, but it was a human emotion, and a human reaction to it.

But something from space?

What did it want?

And what, if anything, could she do about it?

Somehow, she needed to leave the burgh entirely, she couldn't remember why, but it was true. And since that was true, how could it also be that she needed to stay in the spindle, deep in the clutches of the Chapter?

24

TROYLUS

HE JUMPED, HIS HEART HOPPING INTO HIS THROAT AND HIS already labored breaths became great gulping intakes of air.

The big hairy beast of the plain stared at him, from a distance his hand wouldn't have fit in, with all three eyes on that side of its head.

"What are you doing here, friend?" Part of him thought that if Xander heard him refer to an animal whose species they hadn't named yet as friend, he would think Troylus dropped his tether, but it was still true.

It didn't answer, but it huffed out a heavy, hot breath and the hum coming from its chest changed back to the same one it made when he was in the long grass touching it.

Xander was loud coming down from the tree, but he stopped a few branches up and crouched on one while he gripped another with both hands and looked over the side of it at Troylus with the animal, his eyes wide.

"There was a lot of noise, but I didn't expect this," he said gesturing with his head to the large cleared space in front of the tree he was in.

"No, that was after a lot of other things went sideways." Troylus reached out and placed a hand on the section of the beast's hair on its neck that was longer and framed its head.

Hums grew louder, but it wasn't only the animal he was touching doing it anymore. It spread through each of the members of the herd, their hums all the quiet contented kind he now recognized, but with all of them doing it together, the effect was a surreal level of noise for something so innocuous.

"Thank you," he said, looking the one he touched in one of its three eyes, and then looking at the rest of its scattered friends, "all of you."

"Why? What did they do?" Xander asked and Troylus smiled.

"I'm not cold anymore, do you want to walk while I tell you?" he asked.

Xander nodded and finished climbing down from the tree, hopping off the last branch and deciding that move brought him too close to the dark fur of one of the creatures so he took a step back.

Troylus bit his lip so he wouldn't laugh. Xander was actually handling everything pretty well for someone who had not met the beasts the same way he had.

But as they started walking in the direction he knew was toward the spindle and Zellendine, his hairy friend shoved its head under his legs and lifted him onto its back.

"What in the universe does that mean?" Xander asked while Troylus adjusted to get more comfortable. It wasn't half bad.

"It means I don't have to walk, and even though I'm going to be wet still, and smell like this guy." He patted the animal on the neck, "I'm for sure not going to be cold because this fur and giant body is really warm."

Xander actually looked out, like he wanted to ride one too and didn't think he was going to get to.

Until another one did the same to him, tumbling him onto

its back. He tottered and almost fell off but caught himself and got situated more comfortably.

Troylus caught him up on all that had happened and Xander looked both horrified a curious.

"What's that look for? I almost died and you look like a kid playing in the orchard."

"Besides the fact that it's still bizarre you bonded with these guys so much they followed you here and are giving us a ride, I was just thinking that we really need to name all these animals and send a report so people don't wander into some really big teeth."

His laugh surprised him, he didn't think he was going to be able to laugh so soon after believing he wouldn't make it.

"You're right, we do need to name them. What are you thinking?" Troylus asked.

Xander tilted his head and studied the others who were weaving through the thick trees, breaking limbs that got in their way and rubbing against a lot of tree trunks that squealed in protest like they were about to snap.

"Do you remember..." Xander paused and glanced at him, but he schooled his face to not show any of the shock so many others would when someone spoke of memory. "Any of the big animals we were taught about? It was so long ago that we were told the different classifications and that we likely would have to come up with new ones for the planet, so long ago that I don't," he said.

"There's one that I think was big, hairy, and had horns. A yawx or something like that, maybe we could just call them yawx for now, until someone smarter comes up with a better name."

He smiled and patted the neck of the one he was on, "Hello yawx."

An answering uptick in the hum for a second told him it wasn't a terrible idea in their many eyes.

"Okay," Xander said, "A yawx, what about those predators? The silver ones that came together, I think they look like wolves. Those are the only animals I remember at all, which feels weird to say, even now."

"I know." It was all Troylus would let himself divulge to this person who had become a friend. Even on the planet, he didn't trust that the motto of the Chapter, and the consequences of breaking it, wouldn't haunt him.

"So, wolves, then." Troylus smiled at Xander and raised his brows, expecting him to go on naming.

"That's all I've got. I don't even vaguely remember anymore."

In silence they rode, Troylus tried to pull from the depths of memory long denied a name of some animal that could come close to the white fur ball of death and destruction he had come so close to losing to.

But there was nothing. Unless he named it white fur ball of death, and he didn't think anyone was going to agree to that long-term.

"Do you think they've gone outside?" Xander asked after a time so long between words that Troylus was beginning to nod off on the warm back of the yawx.

"If the universe has any fairness to it, no. In this weather, I hope they wouldn't anyway. But I know Zellendine is so looking forward to feeling ground beneath her feet. And I'm afraid they would take her out the first chance they had just to see it and lift her spirits."

He chewed on his lower lip, because the thought of her facing the purple balls of light like the anomaly had spit at her made his stomach flip over and his heart race.

"But if she's hurt, I don't think they would risk it."

All he could do was nod and hope Xander was right.

They both ate a bar while dripping wet and sitting atop a yawx. The animals never seemed to deviate from the path he would have taken to get to the spindle, but it made sense to him that they would know where the strangest thing in their landscape was.

"Where do you think they crossed the mountains at?" he asked looking down at the back of the head of his mount as it rose and fell in rhythm with its steps.

"Probably the same pass we took," Xander said with a yawn.

"But they wouldn't be able to climb those cliffs, which means there has to be another way through the mountains that is more easily accessible to them, and they reached us in that spot which means it couldn't be all that much longer a route." Troylus leaned forward and hung over the animal's face upside down.

"How did you all get here?"

The creature blinked all six eyes twice and huffed out a breath.

"Still can't actually talk, huh?" Xander asked, smiling.

"Very funny. One day, I'll have them show me." He sat up and looked over at Xander who was grinning so broadly it looked like it hurt his cheeks.

"What?"

"I would trade a lot just to see the person in leadership who read the report on how an easy way through the mountains was discovered."

Troylus couldn't help it, he laughed with Xander.

But in the back of his mind he wondered if Rullon had access to any of the reports, and if his dad and his sister knew he had been out of the spindle, wandering around the wild of a whole new planet for what must have been two months.

Indigo would have been jealous, she wanted to see nature so badly.

Rullon, though. Rullon would have been worried to distraction.

He hoped they didn't know.

2 5

ZELLENDINE

THE LIGHT HURT HER EYES. BEING OUT IN THE MIDDLE OF THE main room in her chair meant she didn't have the luxury of her blanket ceiling to block the incessant light in the spindle.

But when she opened her eyes completely, she wasn't in the middle of the main room.

While she was sleeping, someone had pushed her to one side of the big tables in the service.

Corto was puttering around in the service, working on preparing some meal or another.

"Water, please," she said, her voice painful and hoarse.

He whirled around at the sound of her voice and almost fell over in the process. As soon as he took a deep breath and his eyes weren't so wide he scrambled to get something to drink and brought it to her chair.

"You scared me," he said, smiling at her. "Do you need anything else? Food? Medicine?"

She gulped down the drink with a greedy throat and stomach. It growled as soon as he mentioned food.

"Good, I'm almost ready to feed everyone, but I'll get you a bar while we wait." He dashed back over to where he was prepping and brought her back more water and a snack.

Using her good arm, she took the food and ate it down with more water before she bothered to speak again.

"How is Maurice? How is Imogene?" she asked, her voice sounding a fraction better.

"I'm fine," Imogene said, coming up behind her, "But I think I need to work on you." She grimaced and glanced at Zellendine's collar bone, or where it used to be.

"Maurice needs you more right now," she said, trying not to beg to skip over him. She hurt, but Maurice had almost died. And if her injuries hadn't killed her yet, they likely weren't going to.

"Zellendine." Imogene rubbed at her face, her voice tired and exasperated. "Without you to help fix everyone, including him, none of us might make it."

"Trust me when I say that if you weren't there to clean out the toxins running through his system, nothing I was able to do was going to save him."

Imogene frowned, but she stopped arguing and instead pushed her chair closer to the table.

"You're eating, right?" she asked.

A nod and Imogene went to help Corto bring food to the table while everyone else filtered there from whatever task they were doing.

Greetings and checks on how she was feeling were universal as they all showed up, but even though she was happy to be awake enough to eat with them, and thankful for all of them looking out for her, she was preoccupied.

She wanted to check on Maurice, she wanted to run scans, know where he was, check to make sure all her surgery held and that he was on the mend.

But none of that was going to happen until she ate more.

Healing and growing a fetus in her abdomen took a lot of energy and her body was screaming for more energy before she got to work.

"Do any of you know how long we've been on the planet?" she asked.

"Tomorrow will be four months. And some of the other regions are getting their second spindle drops," Corto said, putting her food in front of her.

So she was over four months along, no wonder she had a little hard bump of a belly. It probably didn't show through her uniform yet, but it would in another month.

"Imogene, how long ago exactly did Troylus leave his spindle?" Was he safe? Was he going to miss the entire pregnancy? Her heart thumped harder just thinking about Troylus out in the unknown of the planet.

"Not that long ago. Don't worry, he'll make it here."

But while Imogene tried to reassure her, she kept her eyes on everything but her.

Zellendine shut her eyes and tried to believe he would be okay, that he would arrive with time before she had to name their child on her own.

"The terraforming is done," Samira said, talking to someone else, "So we can start building anytime."

"Done?"

"Should we wait until after the storm passes?"

Questions started flying at Samira as she shook her head and held her hands up to stave them off.

"I'm just relaying information," Samira said.

"No one should go out there." Zellendine wasn't even aware she spoke out loud until everyone turned toward her.

"That happened because of the storm, right?" Samira asked, looking around at the others at the table.

"Of course, that's the only thing that makes sense." Hassan

looked at Samira like she had dropped her tether and at Zellendine like he felt bad for her.

Zellendine shook her head, knowing that what she was about to say might not be believed, and that she had to try.

"Yesterday, we were attacked, it wasn't the storm."

Everyone except Corto looked like the words that came out of her mouth were just a series of random noises with no meaning attached.

"When we were on the ship," she said, taking a deep breath and forcing herself to keep talking, to tell the secret she never thought she would, "An anomaly threw a flag at me, shattered a window, and would have killed me if Troylus wasn't there with his ability."

"And," Corto started, a line appearing between his brows and his mouth pinching. "That purple thing was the same?"

She nodded, the guilt heavy in her mind that something trying to get to her had managed to hurt Maurice, unless he was also like her, someone who was a target for whatever reason.

"Do you think it was after you, or all of you?" Hassan asked, his eyes wide and his body still.

"If it wasn't after me, then whatever the reason this… purple thing, wants me to die, also wants him gone." She swallowed, her throat dried out again.

"But where does that leave us? Some people will never be able to go outside?" Hassan asked, his face barely moving.

"I…" Everyone at the table stared at her while she tried to think up a way to make it better, to take back her suspicions, but even under the weight of their gazes, she couldn't find one, and the truth, the warning of it, was more important than making them feel good. "I don't know."

A silence, heavy and bizarre in its stillness, fell upon them. The pause that engulfed them all seemed like it was waiting for something, as if there was another moment riding within it, one more that was monumental and full of danger.

Banging rang through the air and she jumped, sending pain slicing through her.

"What the fuck was that?" Corto asked.

No one answered, but it happened again.

BRIAR

"WHY?" HE ASKED, FAILING TO KEEP THE PLAINTIVE TONE OUT OF his voice.

"Because," Journo said, placing the lightest touch on his son's uniform sleeve and glancing at the members of leadership milling through the gathering room among all the other people, "Upton needs off this ship, he keeps having episodes, and we think the planet might help."

"You said I would settle with the family, you promised." Briar wanted to grab his dad and hang on, like he did when he was very small and didn't want to be left in his first class, but instead he chewed on the inside of a cheek and refused to let his tears fall.

"And you *will* settle with us, but we need to head there first and get a house. We need to get your brother there with a lot of time before anything is expected of him besides getting used to it." Journo looked like he was in pain, but it didn't lessen the blow of his words.

"So, you're taking the entire family and leaving me behind." Briar couldn't think about not being able to see his family even once in a while. It was too much. All he could think about was the anger. It was safer.

"We are not leaving you behind," Journo said and Briar scoffed, "We're going ahead so everything is ready for you when you get there."

They were leaving him. No matter what spin his dad put on the idea, the simple truth was, he was being abandoned.

"I don't want you all to go. Why can't someone stay behind with me? You could take the kids and Pop could stay with me." There, that sounded reasonable, his dad had to take that compromise.

"Briar, you're asking us to split up the family completely for almost a year more." Journo rubbed a hand along the back of his neck and his eyes were watery.

"You're not going to change your mind, no matter what I say."

"No," his pop said, stepping up to Journo's side and threading their fingers together. Journo looked at his partner with equal parts gratitude and sadness. And Briar didn't want to see it. "We need to do this, and I think that eventually you'll see we made the best choice in a bad situation."

"I…" Briar looked back and forth between them and found his brother and his sister through the crowd, sitting against a wall and both looking exhausted. It hurt his heart. "Fine, but I need some time before I can say goodbye without showing the kids I'm upset."

Journo nodded and Pop gave him a wavering smile before they turned to head over to his siblings.

First, the woman he thought he was going to be partners with turned out to be flawed, then his oldest friend chose her, now his entire family was abandoning him.

Grandpa Kason spoke with Alara by the window, all the people that were brought to the gathering room to hear their region assignments and that they would be on the next set of spindles were milling about.

The only person he had left was Grandpa Kason and he wasn't sure how much he could still trust the old man.

Any minute someone would come and collect him, take him back to the quarters he had been confined to, but for the first time, he didn't mind being locked away from other people.

None of the other people around were worth getting to know. Not if they would just leave eventually too.

Passing through the crowd, Cara, her little one Hamlin held in her arms, stepped out of his way as he neared her.

He straightened his back, lifted his chin, and kept moving.

If no one wanted him there, fuck them, he would make his own way back to his quarters.

Eventually, they would understand like he did. Eventually, they would all know who was worthy of the planet, and who wasn't.

Until then, he just had to wait while they made the mistake of shunning one of their betters.

2 7

ZELLENDINE

"Is it going to get in anywhere?" she asked, her heart pounding, the ache in her collar bone falling in waves in time with it.

"Do you think it's another attack?"

"Where is that coming from?"

"How many completed doors to the outside do we have?"

"Are there any ways to block all the ways in?"

Everyone yelled at the same time, throwing questions into the air instead of directing them at anyone.

"Stop," Imogene yelled, slamming her hands on the table.

No one spoke, but her yell did nothing to settle Zellendine's speeding pulse or slow the chills running over her body.

"Corto, take Zellendine into the wet room, some of you go with them, some of you go be with Maurice and keep your eyes peeled for any purple."

She turned and walked away.

People did what she asked, full of questions just seconds before, they were more than willing to do something, anything, that seemed like a plan.

Zellendine found herself moving as people pushed her chair toward the wet room and at least a door to put between her and whatever was out there.

Ahead of them, Imogene headed to the tunnel at the other end of the main room from the large tunnel opening they had left through to see the cascade.

"Imogene," Zellendine called and she turned around in response, stopped before she had gotten through the doorway, "Don't go out there, it's safer if you stay in here with the rest of us. Please."

"No, I'll be fine." Imogene smiled at her and it made her want to cry, she didn't look scared at all when Zellendine knew how dangerous the anomaly was. "I have silver eyes, remember?"

She turned back to the doorway and slipped around the corner down the tunnel.

"What did she mean about the silver eyes?" Corto asked as they got into one of the wet rooms and took a seat on a bench by the cupboards.

"That's the theory," Zellendine said, rubbing her good hand over her face. "That anyone with silver eyes isn't a target for this thing, because it didn't aim for Troylus. But I don't know how smart that is, and maybe it doesn't care about hurting her if it can get to those of us it doesn't like."

"Is the purple attack thing the reason so many shields were shut on the ship?" Hassan asked, his eyes on his own hands in his lap.

"Yes, or at least I think so."

One by one, the people around her wilted, like being shut into a wet room was somehow the worst possible scenario.

"Why are none of you worried about her?" she asked, finally done with what she thought probably looked like a massive pity party.

"That's not fair," Corto said, "I am worried about her, but this whole thing is shit, right?"

She shook her head, although it made her suck in her breath with a hiss of pain.

He cringed and gave her the sorry face.

"I don't know what you mean, Corto."

"All of us, every person from the Wheel, came across space, some of us never even setting foot on a planet." He gestured to her and she frowned, because it was true, and she thought she knew where he was heading, "Every single one of us has dreamed of this life, has imagined it a thousand times."

"But all of that may mean nothing," Hassan said, still staring down at his hands and Corto threw his hands in the air and held one out toward Hassan as if to say, see?

"Exactly." Corto sighed and went back to looking like someone stole something from him.

Maybe she had.

"Listen, I'm sorry," she said, "I know how much this threat sucks, and I'm hoping I'm entirely wrong, but there has to be a way to deal with it so everyone can still live on the planet. There is no way this is just the end of living on the ground."

"You don't know that," Corto said, his voice quiet and sad.

"And you don't know that I'm wrong. We just have to figure out what the thing is that causes the attacks."

"Oh, just." Corto looked at her like she was a few bars shy of a meal and she wanted to smack him.

"Every damn day I have to work on walking, creating whole new pathways for my brain to communicate with my body, do you honestly think I'm going to let some fucking purple alien light stop me?" she yelled, her good hand clenched in a fist and her bad one feebly grasping the edge of the brace even though it sent pain radiating up her arm.

"It's a purple alien light. How do we know it even has

motive? Maybe you're just really shit at timing when to be where?" Corto yelled back.

"Stop it." Hassan lifted his eyes from his hands to fix a hard gaze on them both. "You two are screaming at each other, in this fucking room of all places, so it bounces around and gets even louder, while Imogene is out there, maybe getting attacked. Just shut up."

Zellendine bit her lip and Corto crossed his arms over his chest before slumping down to lay on the long bench, the others in the room went back to their silence, including Hassan who began studying his hands anew.

But in her mind, the argument still raged, how was she going to figure out what it wanted? And if she didn't, what would that mean for the future on the planet, not just hers?

The wet room might have been the safest place for her at that moment, but what she really wanted was to be out of her chair, even just to lay down in her bed, and have a holo in her hands. At least with a holo, she could have examined herself and Maurice, compared them against Imogene and try to find a file on Troylus to use too.

In the back of her mind she knew there was a pattern, a reason, something she could find, if only she could start looking.

Behind her chair, the door to the wet room opened and Corto popped up from the bench, his hands in fists.

He relaxed, glanced at her, and smiled.

Imogene must have come back.

She let out a heavy breath, at least Imogene was okay.

But a second later someone skidded to a halt in front of her, on his knees, with dirt and twigs in his long hair which was plastered to his head, wet. His uniform was soaked through, and he smelled strange.

None of the details mattered, because Troylus's silver eyes

were more full of love than she had ever seen them, swimming with tears as they were, and his hand was on hers.

He was home.

"Troylus."

2 8

TROYLUS

"OH, ZELLENDINE," HE SAID, LEANING IN TO KISS HER ON LIPS that looked too large for a face thinned to the point of gauntness.

Just past her neck, where her collar bone was, there was a huge, swollen, bruised, and red streaked lump. That arm was in a sling, her hair was greasy and brittle looking, the shine of the blonde dimmed. She was in a kind of chair, adjusted and padded, on skids.

"It was you banging?" she asked, her voice hushed, everything about her was muted except her eyes, the deep, dark brown of them were just as vibrant and full of depth as ever.

He nodded and put a hand to her cheek.

The others were walking away, leaving them alone in the wet room, the questions they peppered Imogene and Xander with filtered through the open door.

But none of that mattered, he had her in front of him. They were together and she wasn't dead.

"Now that I'm here, it won't hurt you again."

She closed her eyes and smiled, her whole body relaxing, as

if she was holding herself together by sheer force of will and now that he was there, she didn't have to.

"I want you to tell me everything, but I think we should both have a wash. I'm freezing and smell like a yawx." He smiled when her brow furrowed.

"What's a yawx?" she asked, making him smile more.

He told her all about his journey while he got a wash ready and with his hands as gentle as he could make them, helped her out of the chair, out of her uniform, and out of her brace, before he put her in the hot water and joined her.

"Will you let me help this?" he asked, running a finger along the skin that wasn't discolored on her shoulder.

"It's shattered, I think I need surgery," she said, her eyes closed and her body braced as if even his light touch hurt.

"How about surgery by blue light?"

"You should help Maurice, he's really hurt."

"I know, and I will, but I won't be able to focus on that, to do the best by him, if I'm thinking about you in pain. Please."

"But we're not sure what it will do to the fetus."

Troylus rolled his eyes and smiled, "I don't think that a fetus with part of my DNA is going to be hurt by my own ability. I promise, I'll only focus on your collar bone."

Zellendine bit her lip and gave his hand a longing look. Finally, she nodded which made her wince.

He pulled on his ability and let it pour out of his hand near her neck, focusing on a whole, well, and strong collar bone that was exactly as it had been. The blue reflected off the water and lit up her face like she was made of it.

She shut her eyes and grimaced, her good hand clinging to his arm.

By the time his ability ran out, there were blank spots in his vision and she was breathing easier. The swollen and bruised area was down to a small lump but it remained discolored and looked sore.

"I'm sorry, I don't think it got everything," he said, his voice frail and weak even to himself.

"No, Troylus, it's so much better, I already know it is." She kept her arm tucked to her side but lifted her other hand from his arm to hold the side of his face.

He leaned into her palm, relishing the fact that she was even there, that he had made it.

"Zellendine, I'm going to find a way to get rid of that damn anomaly. If it kills me, I'm going to make sure you can use that code your dad gave you to send the message and then get you away from the Chapter." He kissed her hand and she sucked in a breath, her mouth falling open and her gaze far away.

"What? What is it?" he asked, yanking on his ability even though he knew there would be no response, because there must have been an injury he missed.

"My father left me a code…" Her eyes returned to his and horror bloomed in them. "There are holes in my memory, and that code is in one. I knew I was forgetting something important."

She squeezed her eyes shut on a tear that trickled down her cheek.

"Hey," he said, taking her good hand and kissing the back of it, "It's okay."

"No," she said, shaking her head, her mouth pinched and turned down in a frown, "It's not okay. My dad died for that code. I have to warn the rest of the ships."

With every word her voice rose and shook more.

"Yes." He grabbed her good shoulder and forced her to look at him, "It is okay. We *will* figure it out. We have time. I don't know how to get rid of the anomaly yet, and that has to come first. You're okay."

She took a deep breath, it hitched and stumbled, but she did it, nodding at the end.

He put his forehead to hers and held her while she breathed.

They washed and cleaned, careful not to over work her injured arm.

"Zellendine, how long has it been since you were able to wash?" he asked, running his hands through her hair. The frailness of it made him wish his ability could return it to its former beauty.

"About as long as it's been since you were able to," she said, a smile on her face.

"Fair." He smiled back. "I mean, I am the one who stunk."

She laughed, and even though her face was too gaunt and the general look of pain and suffering had not left her completely, when she laughed she looked more like herself.

"How is the pregnancy?" he asked, with a pang of guilt that he had waited so long for the question. But, if he was honest with himself, it was the fourth most important thing for him at the moment. She was the first, second, and third.

Zellendine's smile turned rueful and she dropped her eyes to her stomach, a small pouch clearly there.

"I don't even know. It's fine, everything seems healthy in the scans," she said, returning her eyes to his, the odd expression still on her face, "But it sure isn't what I thought it would be so far."

She shrugged one shoulder and laughed, the sound devoid of humor.

"I'm sorry." He wanted to have more to say, the right things to say. But he didn't even know where to begin. "I'm sorry I wasn't here."

Putting her hand on his cheek, she nestled into his side, her breath evening out.

He couldn't let her sleep in the wash, but sleep was something she needed, and nothing sounded better to him than lying next to her.

"Come on, let's go to bed."

She nodded and he helped her from the wash, dried her off, and got clean uniforms from the cupboards.

"In a perfect world, they would have sleep clothes in here, but I couldn't find them." He put her in her chair and shoved it out of the wet room.

"To be honest, I don't remember what it's like to sleep in anything other than a uniform."

Xander and Imogene were talking to the rest of the crew at the tables, but all voices stopped and every eye turned to watch them as they made their way past.

Zellendine pointed when he needed to turn, and directed him to a blanket held back by a hook.

Her room was barely more than a bed draped in blankets for privacy.

"Maybe we can make this a little bigger," he said, looking around and trying to imagine how they would even get dressed next to each other.

"Listen to you. You just got here, and you want to change everything." She smiled at him, her head cocked to the side.

"What I want," he said, scooping her up from her chair and putting her in the bed, "is time with you. I want to spend every day with you."

He climbed in next to her and put a hand on her stomach, his other under his head and playing with her still damp hair.

She smiled, closed her eyes, and kissed him, soft and slow.

"Me too."

2 9

ZELLENDINE

SHE TAPPED AWAY ON HER HOLO WHILE TROYLUS BROUGHT THEM food from the service.

He put a hand on the edge of the holo and raised his brows.

"Time to put it down for little bit," he said.

"I know." She sighed, setting it to the side as the others trickled to the tables for their midday meal.

"Are you recharged?" Imogene asked, sitting opposite Troylus on the other side of Zellendine.

"Not yet, I mean, it's there, but I still feel weak. Have you been able to treat him again?" Troylus asked, referring to Maurice.

"Your friend hasn't let me anywhere near him." Imogene shook her head and took a bite, but Zellendine furrowed her brow and glanced at Troylus.

"I'll talk to him. You and I both should try and help. He doesn't get it, but I can help him understand." Troylus took a bite and stared in the direction of Maurice's room.

She hadn't met Xander yet, he didn't often leave Maurice's side, but she couldn't help wondering what he was like. Because

Imogene was right, he and Troylus were friends. Who was this new person?

There was no reason for her to be suspicious of him, no reason for her eyes to constantly scan the room, for her ears to try to listen to everything, yet that's what she was doing.

And it was exhausting. But as she ate and listened to the conversations around her, she realized why.

Briar. After Briar had become everything she believed he would never be, she had a hard time trusting new people. It took a near deadly accident to learn to trust her own crew.

Zellendine shook her head, it was no way to live. She had to get over it. Especially where Troylus's friends were concerned.

"Are you going to tell me what you're doing?" Imogene whispered, leaning toward her.

She looked to Troylus who lifted his hands in the air in an I don't know either gesture and turned away, leaving her to explain a hunch she didn't entirely have the words for. But she did need Imogene's help…

"I think I might be able to find a marker in my blood that is different than yours or Troylus's."

"Well, that only makes sense." Imogene looked at her like she was wasting time.

"Yes, but what if Maurice has a similar marker? What if we can predict who the purple thing will attack?" The second it was out of her mouth, she knew it made her sound like she dropped her tether.

"Don't you think it's more likely the purple thing is something akin to lightning? Or do you think it's something more? Like it's sentient?" Imogene asked, her voice low and gentle, but no matter how hard she tried to sound like she was just asking a question, Zellendine heard the subtle accusation.

"Listen, I know it sounds like I'm completely off tether, but you weren't there."

Imogene frowned, her face falling into the mask that Zellendine hated seeing on her. The one that said, I'm not going to show you anything.

"Okay, if you want to look into it," Imogene said, sitting back and starting a conversation with the person next to her.

With Troylus engaged in a riotous discussion about the yawx and the names of the other animals, she was left, at the end of the table, with nothing but her own thoughts.

"Hey, do you remember what the predator was that looked like this?" Troylus asked, picking up her holo and tapping at it until he drew an off kilter, and rudimentary cat.

"That's a cat," she said, dead pan. And the table started laughing.

"No, a cat was a small, cute pet." He turned the holo back toward himself and cocked his head studying it. "This thing had giant teeth and claws and was as big as your bed."

"So it was an evil cat," she said.

"Maybe we should just call it evil cat," Corto said, laughing so hard he had to wipe tears from his eyes.

"Come on." Troylus put the holo down and rubbed his face, trying to suppress a smile playing at the corners of his mouth.

He might have stopped himself from giving in to the teasing, but it made Zellendine smile.

"What about venom cat?" she asked, trying to find a less ridiculous sounding way to say evil.

"Fuck, is it venomous?" Corto asked, his good humor gone.

"Maybe not that one then." She shook her head; she should have thought of the obvious way people would take a name like that.

"Snow cat," Xander said, coming to the table and taking a seat.

He looked like he wasn't going to make it through his meal without falling asleep.

"But we weren't in the snow," Troylus said, shoving a plate full of food at Xander who nodded.

"Right, but it was all white." He shrugged and everyone dawned similar expressions, as if they were all trying it out in their heads.

Zellendine was. Snow cat, that didn't sound half bad.

"Plus, it's entirely possible the thing goes up in the mountains where there is snow," she said. "I like it." She smiled at Xander who blinked twice at her and smiled back.

"Snow cat…" Troylus mumbled the name to himself over and over again, his brow furrowed and his attention solely focused on the table in front of him.

Xander raised an eyebrow at him but just continued to chew.

"Wait," Troylus said, too loud and the entire table turned to stare at him as his face lit up. "There were big, dangerous cats we learned about, but they had other names, one of them I think started with snow."

"Does that mean we have a name for the evil toothed white thing?" Xander asked, looking markedly more excited than tired after naming one of the planet's animals.

"Yes, we should absolutely call it a snow cat." Troylus beamed and the others at the table all smiled, witnessing history that even without losing the edict not to look back, all the children and children's children of the planet would learn.

"I don't know," Zellendine said, the entire table turned toward her, only Troylus didn't look annoyed with her, "I kind of like evil toothed white thing."

Everyone smiled, some relaxing as they laughed.

Laughter was good, hearing it, engaging in it. They all needed it, they had experienced too little since her fall.

But the general joviality made her look toward Maurice's room and wonder if he could hear them.

And if he did, what did he think about his crew members having such a good time while he lay in bed, trying to force his body to heal from what could have been a mortal wound.

Over the speakers in the spindle, a chime sounded.

"It might be your spindle, I sent them a report." Corto hopped up front the table and ran to the small alcove the comms had been moved to after her accident.

"I really wish he wouldn't say it that way," she said.

"Say what, what way?" Troylus's mouth quirked up at the corner at his own ridiculous sounding question and she shook her head with a small smile.

"That it's *your* spindle he's talking to. This is your spindle now. We're never going to be assigned different spindles again." She held his hand and he threaded their fingers together.

He lifted their hands to his mouth and kissed the back of hers, neither of them breaking their eye contact until Corto ran back to the table, as white as the snow cat must have been.

"What's wrong?" Troylus asked, releasing her hand and beginning to stand from the table.

"It," he started and had to take another breath before he finished. "One of the damn purple light things that turns solid, attacked someone while they were building a house at one of the other spindles."

She couldn't breathe, and all the small hairs on her body stood up.

"They died. It killed them."

"Did they have silver eyes?" Imogene asked.

Chills rolled in waves down Zellendine's skin, and she knew before he said it.

"No, they didn't."

3 0

BRIAR

"WHICH ONE ARE THEY IN?" HE ASKED, CURLING HIS HANDS INTO fists as they itched to burst into flames.

Grandpa Kason glanced at him and pretended he didn't, going back to staring out the window of the gathering room as the spindles left the ship and separated from each other.

"I'm not sure. I would have to check," the old man said.

Briar tried to remember which ones stayed on the planet. His family was on spindle three, but which position was it in? Were both the first two spindles on the ground? The last two? It made it worse, like this was another fresh punishment he didn't deserve, not to know which one to look for.

"And what's the region like, the one they're settling in?"

Grandpa Kason turned from the window entirely, his mouth open a fraction.

"Didn't you ask your fathers?" He screwed his mouth up to the side like he didn't believe what Briar said.

No sign of trust from Grandpa Kason, of all people, made Briar's ability spark in his palms, but he closed his eyes and shoved it back down.

"You locked me in quarters, remember? I can't say shit to my family because you don't want me to, remember?"

The old man turned away and squared his shoulders, making years of age fall from him in the process, and Briar's fists clench even harder.

"When the time comes, you're going to settle in a beautiful region with many lakes."

Lakes. Grandpa Kason was going to settle him in an area full of water.

He laughed, the sound dark and sharp at the edges.

"And I'm supposed to keep believing this plan of yours if you're going to send me from one kind of lock up to another?" he asked, under his breath, and still Grandpa Kason's gaze scanned the room, as if the few there to watch the launch of the spindles would care what they were talking about.

"No one cares what I say, they all think I've lost my tether, thanks to you." He didn't bother the hide the sneer to go with his false gratitude. Grandpa Kason had fooled everyone, including him, but the old man was far from a fool. And Briar wanted him to know that it wasn't a secret anymore, at least to him.

"Tell me, Grandpa Kason, wise leader of this Chapter." He paused until eyes, shrewd even through the heavy wrinkling of the skin around them and the slightly off color to the whites, met his. "When did you decide Stephen had to go?"

People may have been in the room, but their natural instinct to give Briar a wide berth meant that none of them could have heard the harsh, whispered words, but by the way Grandpa's Kason's narrowed eyes scanned the room, he would have sworn everyone watching out the window was listening. The old man was losing his hold.

"I decided no such thing." His lips didn't move, and his voice was barely audible, but he smiled anyway.

"Did that one hit you differently? That question isn't the kind you encouraged me to ask, is it?"

"You clearly don't recall the messages I gave you."

Briar's smile widened, because he did recall, and now he understood it better, he thought.

He opened his mouth to answer, to remind the old man of the ways he was walked down the path that led to a charred body in a small meeting room. He recognized the leading now, at least. But something out the window drew his attention, and the people around them erupted into shocked gasps.

"What happened?" he asked no one, and he didn't get an answer, but it was clear from the pieces that floated through space in front of the window, disappearing as the ship turned.

One of the spindles didn't make it.

"Did it hit the atmosphere wrong?" a voice from the crowd rang out, over the ones speculating which ship had just been destroyed.

"No, some purple thing came out of nowhere and slammed into it. I've never seen a comet like that," another voice said, louder than the hum of shock running through everyone. That hum was swiftly devolving into grief and something edging toward panic.

People stood, a few getting closer to the window like they were trying to see something that would change the heavy reality of what everyone had already witnessed. A few recoiled from the view, and some ran from the gathering room all together.

It didn't take long for them to remember Grandpa Kason was sitting there. Before Briar was able to form whole words, to think to ask whether his family was safe or not, others started peppering the old man with their own questions.

They pounded the air with their words, with their need for some kind of answer, some kind of direction in a universe that suddenly made less sense. The spindles were so close, the people onboard them just hours away from being able to set foot on the planet they all dreamed of.

Others had called Briar cruel since Stephen's death, he had heard them, but he would never be capable of the kind of cruelty the universe could hand someone. Never.

"Which spindle was that?" he finally managed to ask, the words squeezed past a throat that didn't want to work.

"Everyone, please slow down, I know as much as you do about this, let me meet with leadership and find out more details." Grandpa Kason got to his feet, slowly, and with exaggerated care as if he was afraid to fall down at any moment.

Briar narrowed his eyes and shot to his feet, glaring down at the withered face.

"You don't need anyone's help to answer my damn question," he said, putting emphasis on anyone and help. Maybe the other people gathered around didn't notice the scam, but he wanted Grandpa Kason to know that at least he did.

"I... don't..." The old man looked around and acted confused, but Briar sneered.

"Which spindle was that?" he asked for the second, and much louder, time, speaking slowly and enunciating each word carefully.

Grandpa Kason pulled his head back and his mouth grew pinched while his eyes narrowed a fraction.

The people around them leaned in, equal parts hope and fear painting their faces.

Briar had a second to think how strange it was to hope it wasn't his family, and realize that it was someone's. To save his loved ones, he was hoping for someone else's to die.

It was only a second's hesitation before he leaned in further, his ability itching at his hands to be set free.

"I'm sorry." Grandpa Kason turned to face others looming

over him. "I missed it happen, I don't know for sure which one it was. I need to speak to others who will know. I promise, I will tell you all."

He turned and limped through the group, people stepping out of the way to avoid breaking protocol and touching him.

The old man may have convinced everyone else, but Briar was sure. Grandpa Kason knew, and he was hiding it. What he didn't know was why, when everyone would find out eventually.

3 1

ZELLENDINE

A WAVE WENT THROUGH HER WHOLE BODY, LIKE A SHIVER BUT worse, a tremor. It shook more than her muscles, she felt it deep within her bones.

"It's trying to kill me," she whispered, while the rest of the crew were talking over each other.

Troylus, without her even being aware of him moving, wrapped his arms around her and tucked her into the space between his chin and his shoulder, where her head fit like he was made for her to rest there.

"Nothing is going to hurt you, I promise," he said, his voice raw and harsh, but it managed to soothe the tremors running through her.

"We have to get rid of it," she said, her voice not sounding like her own. She sounded stronger and starker than she normally did.

"I know, we will." He kissed her on the head and she squeezed her eyes shut, unwilling to let herself devolve into the tears pressing against her lids.

"How can we leave here if nowhere out there is safe?" A tear made it past all her attempts at keeping it from falling.

"Zellendine, no matter what we have to do, even if the answer is stay here in the spindle, we will do it."

Troylus took a large, gentle hand, and brushed her hair away from her face, rubbing away the salt water trickling down her cheek.

"But I'm supposed to remember the damn code, and then send the damn message, how can I do that from here?" She clutched at him, the possibility that she would never remember was bad enough, the possibility that she would but not be able to use the code her father died for, was so much worse.

"We'll figure it out. We'll hide it from them." He kissed her head and bit his lip, his arms tightening around her.

"If they catch us," she said, the tremor running through her again at the thought of being put back into space and locked in perpetual cryo alongside Troylus while their child was raised to be the perfect Chapter citizen.

"They won't. I won't let them hurt you again. No matter what." He buried his face in her neck and rubbed his hands along her back, running his fingers through her hair.

She believed him, and it only made everything worse.

Nothing he could do was going to ensure she wouldn't get hurt. But she knew he would try. And in the trying, he could end up being the one to take the fall for anything she got caught doing. In her mind, it started playing like a memory, something so real it felt like it had already happened.

Zellendine sucked down a hitching breath and pulled away from him, tucking all the parts of her that wanted nothing more at that moment than to stay in his arms and weep away where she would allow them room to breathe later.

"Are you okay?" he asked, his eyes searching hers, the silver in them almost glowing like they were lit from within.

She held a hand to his cheek and he closed his beautiful eyes to lean into her palm.

"Yes, I'm going to be. But we have a lot of work to do." She managed to keep steel in her voice and the desperation out of it long enough for him to open his eyes and stare into hers, "And I don't think you're going to like it."

"I already don't like the sound of you saying that." The glowing light went out of his eyes and they went back to their pseudo normal silver.

"Everybody," she said, turning away from Troylus to address the entire table.

Most of them didn't stop their heated conversations, some of them were even still arguing that it could just be a coincidence since most of the population didn't have silver eyes.

"Hey, guys," she tried again, a little louder.

Only a couple more eyes turned her way and she was well and truly pissed off.

"Shut up," she yelled.

All conversation stopped, some mid word.

Imogene looked at her with that stone face only she was capable of, but a tiny muscle in the corner of her mouth twitched and Zellendine was sure she had something to say.

Troylus raised both his eyebrows and bit his bottom lip, trying to repress the smile that wanted to pop onto his face as he scanned the rest of the group.

"Listen, just for a minute," she said, patting Troylus's chest so he released her, moving to crouch at the side of her chair and wrap her hands in his.

"I think I'm the only one of us, besides Maurice, who's had the purple come after them."

A couple heads nodded, other brows furrowed, and some people remained unreadable, while Troylus stiffened at her side.

"But I think we need to know for certain if it's a matter of just those of us without silver eyes that it targets, or if there's something else going on."

"Something else? Are we back to sentient weather?" Imogene asked.

"Yes." She could have sworn she caught someone roll their eyes, but she pressed on. "It may have an explanation though."

Zellendine turned to look at Xander, all the other eyes of the group turned toward him too.

"What?" he asked.

"Xander, when you and Troylus came in from the storm, there were strikes happening on the spindle itself, right? How close did you get to them and did they go after you at all?"

He looked down at the table and his top lip pushed out for a second before he looked back at her and said, "No. And I don't even remember thinking it would."

"Right. So, when I see it, terror runs through me, hot and molten, and when you see it, it barely strikes you as odd."

Xander rubbed his forehead like he was getting a headache.

"Am I supposed to glean something from that besides the fact that you had a traumatic experience once before with it?" Xander asked, not rudely, but like he was trying to understand. "Because if I had been through the situation in the cryo bay with only Troylus to help me, I would probably be scarred for life."

"Says the guy who was up a tree while I was fighting the snow cat," Troylus said, shaking his head and turning back to focus on Zellendine.

"You're right," Zellendine said, directing her words at Xander, "I am not objective. But, if we can figure out that there is something fundamental, DNA level, different about me and Maurice from say you and Imogene and Troylus, maybe we can know who needs to be careful. And maybe, big maybe, we can get a better idea of why this is happening and what's causing it."

"And what's the plan, then?" he asked, still rubbing his face as if he was exhausted.

"The plan has a few phases, first is that I pack all my shit, the next is that I start on the research. I'm going to need everyone to allow me to run scans on you. It won't take long, and I guarantee you've had them before while on the ship."

Nods, everyone seemed to agree, and she knew it was a good idea, but in the back of her mind concerns about causing divisions among the crew that could be misconstrued bothered her.

Chapter computers already decided which babies would survive being born in the mechanical wombs, what would happen if they could identify who might develop abilities?

But for the moment, they needed to know. They needed to be able to protect themselves from their unknown enemy.

Even if it meant delays taking down the enemy they could see in the Chapter.

3 2

TROYLUS

AFTER HELPING SET UP ZELLENDINE IN HER MEDIC ALCOVE, HE kissed her on the cheek.

She didn't even twitch in response, her fingers already rapid fire tapping at her holo.

He smiled and walked away, she had his scans, there wasn't much in the way of additional help he could offer.

Instead of hanging around her while she was busy, he went to Maurice's room on the way to the comms.

Without the homes being built in the burgh, he needed to check in with Rullon and Indigo about the delay in them getting to the planet.

But first, he needed to check on Maurice, and talk Xander into letting him and Imogene to use their abilities.

It made no sense for him to try and stop help, no matter where it was coming from.

The room Maurice was in was as makeshift as anyone else's but Xander had hung a piece of rope across the pseudo door like the world's most useless lock.

He ducked under the rope and shoved his way inside, blinking into the dark as his eyes adjusted.

Maurice was asleep in the small bed, his body bandaged, and his lined face as relaxed as Troylus had ever seen it.

Xander must have hung more blankets across the ceiling to block out the lights. The room was even darker than Zellendine's, little light got past the edges of the blankets, and Troylus didn't think that was how Maurice would have had it.

"Hey," Troylus said, after a few seconds for his eyes to adjust, "Maurice. How you feeling?"

As quiet as he tried to be, his words still seemed too loud in the solemnity of the dark.

Maurice didn't flinch at the sound of his voice, his breathing remained steady and deep, deeper even than could have been comfortable with his remaining injuries.

Troylus grabbed one of the blankets overhead and yanked it down, leaving the other drooping, but still blocking the light from shining directly into Maurice's face.

He looked fine.

If Troylus ignored the bandages, he never would have guessed how close Maurice had been. But something about his old friend's condition bothered him. It tickled at the edges of his mind, that something was off.

Poking his head out of the doorway, he spotted Xander still at the table, talking with a few others while he continued to eat his meal, resting his cheek on one hand.

The guy was exhausted, how long had he stayed awake, sitting in the dark with Maurice?

Zellendine was still in her chair, in the alcove, surrounded by her medic equipment, most of which Troylus had never seen her use and wasn't even sure what it was for.

He bit his lip and glanced back at Maurice, he didn't want to interrupt her, especially so soon after she started on her research, but Maurice needed someone who could recognize what was actually wrong with him.

And as much as he trusted his gut on this, he wouldn't have called it diagnostic.

Before he could take even two steps in Zellendine's direction, Imogene popped up in front of him, rubbing at her eyes. Even though she was heading in to see Maurice, Troylus thought she needed to be getting some sleep instead.

"I didn't think you were heading back in here," he said, following her and deciding to ask Zellendine later.

"Well," she said, with a heavy sigh as she perched on the edge of a chair next to the bed and looked at Maurice, "Xander is still eating, so I thought it was the perfect time to try using my ability."

He repressed the urge to say good, but he did grin.

"Yeah, yeah, you brought it up so I was paying close attention," she said, rolling her eyes and leaning forward.

Placing her hands a fraction above the wrapped wound, she closed her eyes and called on her ability.

Yellow light flowed from her, not the torrent it was in space, the almost uncontrollable flood, but soft waves, strong and steady.

Maurice squirmed and writhed, his mouth opened on a silent scream.

Troylus stepped forward to tell her she could stop, but she slumped to the side first, the yellow no longer lighting the small room.

"Hey," he said, touching her on the shoulder and leaning over Maurice, who panted but still didn't wake up. He wasn't sure who he was addressing, or which one could hear him.

"Imogene," he said and she blinked up at him. "Oh, good. Listen, I have to get Zellendine, are you okay?"

"Yeah, fine. Go," she mumbled, curling her legs up and settling into the chair, her eyes fluttering back to shut.

He ran from the room, skirting the edge of the main space, close to the railing around the hole in the center to get to the medic alcove as fast as he could. Maurice should have woken up, something was very wrong.

"Zellendine," he said when he reached her, shoving his hand between her and the holo, grimacing as he braced himself for how pissed off she would be.

"Troylus?" She blinked up at him, her mouth turned down in a frown, "What are you doing?"

"I need you to come examine Maurice, please."

She glanced in the direction of Maurice's room and to where Xander was still at the table, seemingly half asleep.

"Okay, let's go," she said.

He shoved at her chair, and got it moving, every second more frustrated that he couldn't make it go faster.

They rounded the corner into Maurice's room, Imogene and Maurice both asleep.

"Maurice didn't wake up even though he was in pain while Imogene worked on him," Troylus said, moving around her chair to pull her a fraction closer to Maurice's side.

"But isn't that good? Her didn't feel the pain?" she asked, taking her holo back out and starting to tap at it, glancing back and forth between it and Maurice, prone on the bed.

He took a deep breath and smiled, he knew she wouldn't wait for his answers.

"I don't know, honestly, but something is really weird. It seems like he should have woken up if he was going to show the pain on his face, and…" he trailed off, looking at his old friend.

"And what?" she asked, making eye contact with him, ignoring the holo in her hand for a second.

"Something about it sets off every alarm bell I've got."

Zellendine looked back to Maurice and nodded, before she dove back into her holo.

It only took a few moments before her mouth fell open and she sucked in a loud, hissing breath.

"What?" he asked, rubbing the back of his neck.

"His scans say he's in the same kind of solid REM as the sleepers were," she said, lowering the holo in her hands to her lap and starting at him.

"But that…" he couldn't finish his sentence, and he didn't need to. She knew, they had said it too many times since their last shift. It was still true, and they still had to deal with it.

But he wasn't wrong.

It didn't make sense.

3 3

BRIAR

IT WASN'T HIS FAMILY'S SPINDLE, HE KEPT REPEATING IT TO himself, locked in his quarters.

At least they had allowed him to hear that bit of news, though he stopped them from telling him more.

He didn't want to know who was onboard the doomed spindle, he didn't want to think about the people who died as he wished for them to so his family could live.

They could have been people like him, the whole spindle could have been full of the very people who were supposed to settle the planet, the very people he did everything for.

But the faces of people he didn't even know, faces he saw once or twice in the hallways as they passed each other in too close proximity, kept running through his head.

Who was missing their brother? Upton flashed behind his eyes.

Who was missing their sister? Rhea's face appeared in his mind.

Who was missing their parents? Both of his fathers, holding

hands and looking at him in one of their proud moments, floated around in his mind's eye.

Pain, sharp and jagged, ripped through his heart. If they had died, they would have gone to the stars still thinking he had done wrong, still thinking nothing he had done was justified.

Somehow, he needed to get to comms. Somehow, he needed to be able to convince them that his actions were the righteous ones.

A mission formed in his mind, swirling among the images of his family members.

Having his family to fuel him, having his mission formed, whole and complete in his mind, meant that it didn't matter how long it took for him to get out of this damn room.

When he did get out, nothing was going to stop him.

But first, he needed to get to comms.

34

TROYLUS

"Uh, guys?" Xander asked, standing in the doorway with one eyebrow high, it looked like he was silently counting how many people were shoved into the space.

"Maurice is asleep," Troylus said, looking past Zellendine's chair while she kept tapping at her holo and didn't seem to notice Xander was even there.

"I know, I figured it was good for him to stay that way." He gestured with his head to the curled up Imogene. "Did she do another round with her ability? How did he take it? I was hoping to give his body time to rest between rounds of being hit with that."

"No, I mean," Troylus said, and caught him up on everything, Xander's face falling more and more into shock as he spoke.

"But that doesn't make sense," Xander muttered and Troylus glanced at Zellendine who didn't look up, but a corner of her mouth quirked up for a second.

So, she was listening, even if she was too busy to respond.

"We know. But she's running all kinds of scans before we try anything else." Troylus turned to look back at Maurice and wondered if all he had to do was wait until his ability was all there without any remnants of it feeling tired, then kiss Zellendine.

It worked last time, and he was more than willing, but somehow he thought his ability had caused Maurice's current condition. And if that were true, the last thing he should do was use it again.

"How did she get the sleepers on the ship to wake up?" Xander asked, looking at the back of Zellendine's head.

She looked up at Troylus and sighed before she turned in her chair to look at Xander out of the corner of her eye, making Xander jump like he thought she was asleep too.

"The way we woke them isn't going to do us any good now. We used an ability, and I think that's clearly out of the picture right now," she said, turning back around and focusing solely on her holo.

Xander rubbed his hands over his face and his mouth pinched as he took in Maurice in the bed and Imogene in the chair.

"Is Imogene okay?" he asked.

"Yes, but we should probably get her to her room so she can really rest."

Zellendine nodded and Troylus and Xander went about moving her chair out of the room and carrying Imogene to her bed. She didn't wake up.

But Troylus knew the feeling of draining yourself too much, and he knew she would be fine. It was Maurice he wasn't sure about. It was Maurice who was another mystery for them to understand.

As they neared the door to Maurice's room again, where Zellendine waited, continuing to work the problem the way she knew best, Corto came sprinting around the corner of a wall made of stacked boxes and almost slammed into them.

"What in the universe? Slow down," Xander said.

But Corto bent over at the waist, trying to catch his breath, with a hand raised in the air.

He stood back up again, his eyes wild, and said, "There's been a bad accident with one of the spindles making a drop off of passengers."

Troylus felt his stomach sink into his feet, somehow he knew before Corto could say it.

"It was destroyed, everyone on board is gone. Something purple hit it."

"Purple," Xander said, looking at Troylus, his eyes almost as wild as Corto's.

He could only nod.

"Any silver eyes on board?" Xander asked.

"Not that I know of, but the only people talking about that part of the story are all the spindles on the ground. Everyone is asking the family members of the people onboard if they did."

Troylus nodded again, hating that they all knew what they were going to find. He looked past Corto's shoulder to where Zellendine sat and wanted to hide her.

"We should tell Leadership that no other spindles should go on or off the planet unless someone with silver eyes is on it. I know it makes us sound like we should meet with the medics about some scrips to stop delusions, but we have no choice."

He looked back at Corto and Xander who both looked like they were going to be sick, but Xander nodded.

"I'll do it," Troylus said, making Corto let out a big breath and Xander's lip thin into a line. "They already don't entirely trust me. Let's just hope they believe me enough to do as I suggest."

"Do we know which region they were headed to?" Xander asked.

"Yeah, the one you guys just came from," Corto said.

"Shit," Troylus said as he and Xander both started running at the same time, headed for the comms which was deserted. Whoever was sitting there with Corto and got the news was probably delivering it to everyone.

They managed to get the comms going and waited for it to connect with the spindle on the other end.

Eventually, the holo popped to life, still too messed up as it tried to form the face of the person on the other end. Simple reports could go through, and real comms from the ship in orbit worked, but the connection between them and other spindles was too tenuous.

"Hey, who am I talking to?" Obie asked on the other end, his voice sad and dejected.

"Troylus and Xander. Hey, Obie," Troylus said, frowning as he wondered how hard it was for everyone there at the moment. "How are you doing?"

Obie laughed, a humorless sound that was so opposite his personality it was painful to hear.

"We've all been better." Obie told them who had lost relatives, and what some of the people heading their way were assigned to do, but the thing that made Troylus squeeze his eyes shut and bite his lip, was that there were two children on the spindle.

All three of them exchanged updates, including their warning not to let any of the people without silver eyes go anywhere without someone near them with his eyes.

"But we were fine for so long, why is this happening now?" Obie asked.

Troylus shook his head, he had no idea.

"It may be that after the encounter in space, the thing thought it made its point, or didn't realize we would be landing on the planet. It may have just taken it a while to find us and get mad," Xander said with a shrug.

He looked at Xander while his mouth fell open, the same guy that had argued against the theory of why the purple thing attacked, seemed fully in agreement now. Troylus couldn't decide if it was a good thing, or if it was tragic.

"Okay," Obie said, his voice a sigh.

They said their goodbyes and Troylus went back to Zellendine, Xander in tow.

When they got there, she wasn't in her chair.

Looking at the alcove on the other side of the main room, she wasn't there either.

"Zellendine?" he asked, but the giant space didn't answer, and neither did she.

35

ZELLENDINE

Maybe taking herself to the wet room was a bad idea. But she needed to go, and no one was around. Besides, she needed to get in work on her legs and Troylus's healing really had done a lot of good, all she needed to do was work on her strength and her balance. That wouldn't happen from her chair.

But by the time she was done using the wet room, she had to sit along the edge of a wash and rest. Her knees and ankles felt wobbly, her muscles almost quivered from exhaustion, and there was sweat collecting in every bend of her body.

She took another breath, grasped her holo tight as she pushed up with her legs, locking her knees into place once she was upright.

With one hand along the wall, she made her way out of the wet room.

It took a painfully long time for her to shuffle her way along the curving wall to the service.

Looking at the distance between the wall and the table, she tried to imagine the number of steps it would take, to judge if she would make it or if it would be better to slide down the wall and sit there while she continued to work.

But she didn't want Troylus to find her collapsed on the floor, he would only get more protective, and hover more.

She loved him, but she wanted to be able to get back to feeling like she did before. She wanted him, she didn't want to need him.

But first, she had to figure out how to get to the table.

If nothing else, maybe she could crawl.

Pushing off from the wall, she made her way, one careful, shuffling step at a time, until she collapsed onto a bench at the table, almost dropping her holo in relief.

As her belly grew, it would only get more difficult for her to keep her balance. She needed to build up her strength while she could.

Somehow, she was going to have to balance that with her need to help Maurice.

On the holo she had the scans she did of him, Troylus, Imogene, and herself.

What was strange was that while she could see the difference between her own and those of Troylus and Imogene with a quick glance, Maurice's looked more like hers than theirs, and yet it wasn't exactly the same.

No one had exactly the same DNA as another, but he had some of the same markers they did, while his DNA remained made up of the same exact building blocks hers was, not the added unknowns the other two had.

But it didn't matter how long she looked at it, and what new angle from which she compared the scans, nothing explained it.

Finally, she looked at an image of Troylus's blood and she almost fell off the bench.

Troylus sprinted up to her side and pulled her into him, making her drop the holo on the table.

She hugged him back while he dragged in thick breaths and shivered.

"What's the matter?" she asked.

"You were gone," he said, his voice heavy and thick with what sounded to her like sorrow.

"I needed to use the wet room, but I only got this far coming back. But why are you so sad?"

"Fuck, Zellendine." He shook his head with a small laugh.

"Seriously, Troylus, it has to be more than just me not being in my chair." She rubbed her fingers on his back where she was wrapped around him.

He told her about the destroyed spindle, and his conversation on the comms.

A kiss was all she could give him, the only thing she could offer to heal his wounds the way he had healed hers. It wasn't enough, but he relaxed into her embrace.

"I need to find Xander and tell him where you are. He was worried too," he said, kissing her on the cheek and standing from the table.

"Wait," she said, grabbing his arm before he ran off, "When you find him, I need to see him."

"No problem," he said, leaning down and giving her a lingering kiss, his hand on her cheek.

She watched him run off, and while she felt bad for the people in the spindle and their families, she could only be grateful that she had him. Her father was gone, her mother had been gone so long she never expected to have her on the planet, but whatever she had expected from her time on the planet, she never expected to have Troylus.

Movement in her stomach made her gasp and put a hand to the hard knot there while she looked down at her abdomen.

Taking her eyes off her belly and focusing back on her holo

where her scans of Troylus were up, possibilities ran through her head.

Under no circumstances did she want to ask any of the medics still on the ship, but maybe Xander would know how to answer her questions.

He and Troylus arrived not much later as she was pouring through the scans of other members of the crew that she had from their time on the Wheel.

"You know," Xander said, sitting on the bench across from her while Troylus took a seat next to her and wrapped an arm around her back to rest on her hip. "I don't think you'll listen to me, but it's a lot safer for you and the fetus if you only do your physical work to get better while someone is around."

"I know," she said, waving a hand and he raised an eyebrow with a smirk, "Listen, this is important. First of all, I need to do a scan on you, and I need you to help me do new scans on everyone else too."

"Um, why? And wait, that's just the first thing?"

"Because, I think I found something, but I need to be sure so I need everyone's information. And yes, I have more. Second, I need to have you walk me through how I get the same level of scans on the fetus." Troylus stiffened at her side and Xander glanced back forth between them, his brow furrowed.

"Do you think there's something wrong?" Troylus asked, his voice hushed and careful, like him asking the question was going to cause it to be true.

"No. Everything with the pregnancy is fine. I want to know if the fetus has your new DNA or just my old kind, or if they're some kind of mixture. I need to know if they'll be safe from the purple."

He put his forehead to hers and kissed her.

Xander coughed into his hand and Zellendine smiled.

"Can you do that?" she asked, looking back across the table.

"Yes, I can, although there's a couple things that we might only know after birth, but most of it we can get."

She took a breath and grinned at Troylus. Perfect.

3 6

TROYLUS

HE PUSHED THE BUTTON HE COULD BARELY MAKE OUT ON THE WALL in the tunnel, a massive panel in the ceiling lowered in front of him.

Troylus looked back at the large opening to the main room, making sure the huge makeshift doors were closed.

Imogene next to him stepped onto the platform and he joined her with Corto and two others.

"You sure we'll be okay up there?" Corto asked.

"Positive," Troylus said looking up as Corto pushed the edge of the tiny disc in his hand, triggering the panel to raise back up with all of them on it making adjustments, shuffling their feet in the strange feeling.

As the panel lifted, the sun shining above them kissed Troylus's skin, feeding him warmth and fresh air.

Humming came from one side of the large clearing they were in where only a small portion of the spindle showed through the ground anymore.

"Do you really think it's done enough to build on?" Imogene asked, looking down her nose at the ground just past the panel.

"It better be," he said, walking past everyone to be the first to step foot on this section of the planet.

When he and Xander came to the spindle the first time, the yawx, their feet sinking a few inches into the muck, walked them through the clearing on their backs and dropped them off at the edge of the spindle.

Now, he walked through what seemed like solid ground toward the hum in the trees.

Yawx poked their heads past the edge of the trees, but there were more deeper in the woods.

The big one, the one he knew the best, walked all the way out of the trees and blew hot breath in his face while three of its six eyes stared at him from its turned head.

"Hey," he said, smiling, and feeling stupid because he was happy to see the big ugly thing.

"We're going to build some things here for a while, for them." He gestured behind him, "To live in. It might get loud, so if you want to head out for a while and take naps or whatever, I'll understand."

Someone behind him whispered to someone else and he could have sworn he heard the word tethered, but the animal lowered its head and turned around.

All the yawx went back into the trees, the sounds of their movement through the forest more obvious now that he was closer, and yet he still marveled at how little noise they made since that first time he saw them among the trees and they saved him.

He turned to find every single member of the cleared building party, staring at him.

"Fine, it's weird, but we should be good neighbors. And trust me, they're well worth getting to know."

All of them still looked at him like he was imagining things, but he knew, and Xander would have laughed because he knew too.

"Can your new friends do anything about the purple?" Corto asked, and Troylus got the impression he wasn't entirely joking.

"Not that I'm aware of?" Troylus shrugged and Imogene laughed, setting off the others.

"Okay, so how do we plan on getting started out here?" Imogene asked, hands on her hips as she turned to take in the whole of the clearing.

"You're with me," Troylus said, gesturing to her and narrowing his eyes at the section of the spindle still above ground.

"And what am I doing with you?" Her deadpan delivery cracked him up, but she thinned her lips into a line as he explained what his plan was.

"But how would that help protect the spindle?" she asked, while the others were making their way to the edge of the woods and started assessing the trees before they decided which ones they would take and use for their building.

"I think the more we can get covered by the planet, the better it will be, but it's just a theory." He lifted his hands and raised his brow at her, waiting for her to do the same.

She finally did, turning to the raised area.

"What are we going to do with the materials, they shouldn't be wasted, we can use them on the building," she said.

"Good, let's turn it into sheets so we can use it however we need."

He drew on his ability, it was aching to get out, it had been so long, and half a second later, his blue light was joined by her yellow.

The light looked oddly gentle as it tore apart the metal, wires, and other materials, fusing them all together into an amalgamation that they flattened into the same kind of sheets he had created out of the ore.

She followed his lead in the general shape and size, both of them dropping off the sheets in a stack to the side.

It took less energy for him to form these sheets than it did from the raw ore. All the materials they were using were already shaped and used, which meant it was felt more natural to 'fix' it in the way they were.

Finally, his light grew thin and he put his hands to his sides before he dropped to one knee, his head spinning.

Imogene, clutched at her stomach and sat down in the dirt, blinking like she was dizzy.

He nodded at her, although it sent his head spinning.

Of all the people there, she understood exactly what he felt. It made it easier for some reason he couldn't explain, when he needed to lay down on the ground, staring up at the pink striped sky.

"Do you think the pink in the sky is a warning that the purple is watching? It wasn't around the other spindle," he said, not bothering to try and hide his theory, no matter that someone was going to think him even more untethered than usual.

She turned to the side and looked at him, her face a mask that he still couldn't read even after all the time he had known her.

"I have no idea about the purple, I've never even seen it." Her voice was low and the trepidation in it made him look back to the sky, and send a plea to the universe that it wouldn't show up.

Nothing but the pink streaks in the sky to make him worry.

He closed his eyes and listened to the sound of the others felling trees and starting the process of prepping the wood for their builds.

Somehow, it felt like he needed to get the burgh underway as fast as he could. It felt like he was up against a clock to get Rullon and Indigo settled.

But maybe that was Zellendine's growing belly.

37

ZELLENDINE

Her steps were still not as strong as she wanted. It was still a struggle to make it across the main room to the service to get a drink.

The process of standing long enough to get something left her leaning on the counter and her knees quaking.

She guzzled down her drink and started to move, careful to fully lift her feet each step of the way, to the table.

Grasping onto the table with one hand, she pulled her holo out of the satchel at her side.

"Ah, back to work already?" Xander asked, sitting across from her and glancing at the holo in her hands. "Is the satchel working?"

"Yes, it's a big help for my arms to be free. My balance is not improving," she said, shaking her head and looking at her belly. "And of course I'm working, if I just sit around until they come back, I'll lose my tether."

"So, do you have enough to say what caused all the abilities to pop up?" he asked, leaning forward and looking at her holo although she hadn't brought anything up on it yet.

"No." She rubbed at her forehead while she tapped on the holo and brought up her discovery so he could look at it with her.

"I can't believe it's that clear. Why didn't we see this when we were on the ship?" he asked, squinting at the blood cell she isolated from Troylus's sample, so that it twisted in the air above the holo, in three dimensions.

"When I looked at the scans my," she paused and swallowed before she mentioned him, "father did, it wasn't even something he looked at. He was looking deeper, and that's where we saw some changes, but this is so obvious."

She shook her head and he reached out to tap the image, bringing the thin line in the cell into a closer focus.

"Is it just a trick of the holo, or do you think the silver is actually representative of what the cell looks like?" he asked, his voice low and almost reverent, it reminded her of her father when he was deep in his medic brain.

"Under the microscope, it looks like a red blood cell with a silver sliver in it."

He looked up from the holo to furrow his brow at her, gone was the intrigue at something interesting in his field.

"You looked at a microscope? I didn't even know we had one," he said.

"Of course we have one. We have all the old equipment. These spindles were first outfitted, or at least some were, before our great great grandparents left their planet." How did he not know that?

But she answered her own unasked question as he talked about the equipment he had only ever heard of and if they had that too. They did. And she realized that she knew more about the spindles, and all they included, because of Troylus.

It was one more reason that it didn't make any sense for the

Chapter to keep the knowledge of each assignment so siloed away from the other crews.

She shook her head. Thinking about why the Chapter did things, made her want to pull her hair out.

"Oh," she said, her stomach heaving from the inside out like it was an alien thing that no longer belonged to her.

"Kicking?" he asked, tapping something else on her holo and not looking up at her.

"Yes, it's happening a lot now that I'm trying to get up and walk more."

"Have you ran a scan on yourself, not just on the fetus?" he asked, lifting his eyes to hers.

She bit her lip.

"I… I haven't done a scan on the fetus yet either."

"What?" His hand froze halfway to getting to something else on the holo. "Zellendine, that's not safe. We need to do regular scans on the fetus."

"Yes, but if something is wrong…" She turned away from his too piercing gaze, from the judgement there, and tried to find the words to explain the thought process that went through her mind every time she started on the scans.

"I have my scans from a while ago, my blood sample, they haven't changed. I know that at a very fundamental level my DNA is now different from Troylus's. It was when we got pregnant. At this point, are we the same enough for this fetus to be healthy?"

She rubbed her hand over her belly, trying to find a connection to the fetus inside her that she had been holding at bay since she started thinking through everything.

"The thing is, I'm not sure I want to know how different this fetus is to me, or to him. I'm not sure I want to know if my body is incompatible with my own would be child."

"Zellendine, that isn't how that works, if we know anything that is a challenge for you in carrying this pregnancy, we can mitigate that. There are things we can do for almost anything." His voice was careful and slow, the same detached and yet caring way that her father put on when he was talking to patients.

It made her miss him, and like Xander more, even though she saw it for what it was.

"I know it sounds strange, because I know it's not rational, but I don't think I would be able to handle it if there was something so wrong with me that the fetus didn't make it." She looked down at her hands, bringing them to rest on the table in front of her.

"On the ship, during our last shift, there was a terrible thing that happened to a baby as it was being born from one of the mechanical wombs. The mother, she…" Zellendine saw in her mind Yanna in the hallway, Yanna in the gathering room, Yanna at the chute. And Anders, as he looked on, holding it together, and then not.

"Anyway, neither of the parents were well afterward, and I'm not even sure if they will remain partners, or if their lives will ever be the same again. I don't know if I could handle thinking about them while I wondered if the same was going to happen to me and Troylus."

He stretched across the table and placed a hand on hers, his touch feather light.

She looked up and met his eyes.

"Maybe we should run the scans, and I will only tell you what you need to know, I promise I won't tell you any of the things you don't want to know."

Frowning, she thought about it. It formed a lump in her throat to even get that close to knowing the answers, but she looked at him and nodded. He wasn't wrong.

"But," she said, raising a hand as he started to get up from the table with a smile on his face, "I mean it. I don't want to know anything, and I really don't want Troylus to know either."

He smiled, and nodded, holding out a hand for her holo.

"You're doing them right now?" she asked, her voice squeaking.

"We are behind. I need to do them right away." Her gestured again for the holo on the table and she chewed on the inside of her cheek as she handed it to him.

"Okay, so you know how this works, it won't take me long, and at the end of it, I'll only tell you what you need to know." He tapped at the holo as he came around the table to her side.

She took a deep breath and closed her eyes, sending a wish into the universe that everything would be fine.

38

BRIAR

"You have been given an assignment, yes," Alara said, her silken voice barely hiding the irritation he heard plain in it, "But you will remain on this ship for a while yet."

He curled his hands into fists at his sides and stared just over her shoulder at the wall of his quarters, lest she read his thoughts too clearly on his face. If he filled his mind with thoughts of the wall, she wouldn't intuit shit from their conversation.

"I have spent time in cryo, I have spent time in the confines of my quarters, I should have been one of the first people on the ground, studying the planet and the terraforming potential, but instead you tell me I need to waste away here longer?" His voice was like acid, burning through the walls.

"Briar, you killed a man." Her voice still had that smooth and beautiful quality to it, but he would have rather heard anything than her at that moment.

Nothing he said was going to change the Leadership's decision, nothing he said was going to make her listen to him.

So, he sat there and ground his teeth together, his fists

clenched so tight his knuckles popped as he strained to keep his abilities locked inside himself.

"When do I get to go to the planet?" he asked, surprising himself with how calm he sounded under the circumstances.

"You will spend an entire year on the Wheel longer than the spindles."

It took him a minute, he had to think through what exactly that meant.

"Are you saying I will be leaving the Wheel a year after the spindles first left?" he asked, taking his eyes off the wall and turning them on her, hating that he had to ask for clarification, but this was too important. And if she was going to try and make him feel stupid with her word games, he wasn't going to give her the satisfaction of seeing it bother him.

"Yes, Briar." Her eyes narrowed just a fraction and it took everything in him not to respond. "I want you to understand, I advocated for you to have a much harsher sentence."

"Grandpa Kason went to bat for me," he said, because there was no reason for him to hide what he knew.

But her eyes popped open more before they settled almost immediately back to her natural state of looking superior. Whatever he thought her reaction was going to be, it wasn't to be that surprised.

"Actually, you should know, most of the reason you were spared was because of the information Troylus and Zellendine gave us."

With their names, heat poured through his body, leaving goosebumps in its wake and a tremor running through his arms while he fought to keep his ability in check.

"I owe them nothing. They owe me," he said, through a jaw clenched shut.

She watched him as he battled himself, until he was calm enough to relax his stiff back.

But the second he did relax she lifted a brow and said, "Make it out to be whatever you want in your own mind, but the reality is that you would still be in cryo if not for them."

He returned to his struggle for control, although it wasn't as bad this time without their cursed names floating through the air to poison it.

Alara waited, her face growing more smug, and it made it even harder for him not to lash out. None of them deserved the world they were living on, none of them deserved to have what he didn't. The fact she didn't understand that when she was supposedly so wise made it worse.

One more deep breath and he had his ability tethered, the flames were only a dull roar in the back of his mind.

"Grandpa Kason advocated for you to be put into cryo after the spindle disaster," she said. "If he had his way now, you would be heading to a cryo bay to live out the rest of your days instead of going to the planet in a few short months." Her brow lifted a fraction as his mouth dropped open.

"Maybe you should reexamine who you owe what to," she said, turning and walking from his tiny quarters, the door shutting behind her.

Briar turned off the lights in the room, and in the dark, fire flared to life in his palms.

39

ZELLENDINE

"But you said yourself," she said, grabbing onto Troylus's arm and stopping him mid step, "Your ability will protect me."

"I said that for after the baby comes." He ran his hands through his hair and she planted hers on her hips.

"What the fuck?" For a little while she didn't feel the ache in her legs from all the walking she had already done that day, and she didn't feel the strain in her back from her growing belly. All she felt was rage.

"What?" he asked, looking around and dropping his hands from his head like the damn blanket walls were going to give him an answer to explain why he was an ass.

"So you're okay with risking my safety when I'm not pregnant but not while I have your child tearing apart my insides?" she yelled, her voice as harsh as any attack from an ability. He could heal and fix things, she could hurt someone with words.

He winced and tried to reach out to her while he was shaking his head.

"Don't fucking touch me right now."

Troylus threw his hands up palm out and took a step back his eyes huge and his breath coming too fast.

"Okay, Zellendine, that's not what I meant. At all. I love you," he said, slowly moving his hands to either side of her shoulders, keeping them hovering a hair's breadth from her skin.

"If only I was the one with the ability," she said, eyes narrowed and voice cold.

"What I meant was that I don't know how to protect you both right now. I don't know how I would..." His voice broke and he took in a shuddering breath, his eyes lowering to the floor in front of her feet and his hands dropping to his sides.

The rage filled ice in her broke as his voice did.

She reached out and put her hands on his chest.

He scooped her to him, wrapping her tight in his arms, his body bowing around her stomach, and burying his face in her neck.

"Zellendine." His voice was soft, more a vibration on her skin than full words in the air.

"You are such a pain in the ass," she said, bringing a hand up to cup the back of his head and tangle her fingers in his hair.

"Thanks," he said with a laugh, rubbing his hands along her back.

"I can't even stay mad at you when you say something truly, all the way, stupid." She shook her head as much as their position would allow her to.

He pulled back from her and planted a kiss on her mouth, deep and raw with his love for her, she melted into him.

"Come here," she said, tugging on his hand as she stepped back to the edge of the too small bed they shared.

Even though he should have been heading to the second half of his long work day building some of the last of the burgh, he lowered her onto the bed and himself beside her, cupping her face with one hand as he kissed her and ran a hand down her side with the other.

And even though she had work to do checking on Maurice, working with Xander to find a way to wake him up, she clutched at his clothes and hers until they were both as naked as the night before in the wash, and they both forgot about the time.

By the time they were laying in each other's arms, Troylus still trailing kisses up and down her neck, they were more than late to their assignments and she knew it would not go unnoticed.

"Maybe you should tell the builders I was sick again like this morning or that we thought I was having contractions but it turned out to be a false alarm," she said, turning to the side to catch his mouth with her own and sighing.

"They can just shut up," he said, his voice rough and deep, it made her kiss him more fully.

"Stop it," he said, not breaking away from her mouth and going back to kiss her again with a growl.

"You're a terrible influence," he finally said, pulling back and giving her a peck before he climbed from the bed and put his uniform on.

"Oh, well, if I'm terrible, maybe I should just sit here and stay out of trouble," she said, leaning up on her elbows and smiling at him.

He looked down at her, his gaze going from her eyes down to her feet and back again before he growled and leaned down to kiss her again, hard.

Getting back up to standing, he kissed her large round belly and handed her the makeshift smock she had to wear since the uniforms that fit the rest of her body got nowhere near close enough to close over her belly.

She put it on and he ran his hands through her hair, getting the tangles out in the gentlest brushing.

"I love this wild hair," he said, kissing her neck from behind and wrapping his arms around her with his hands on her stomach. "And I love you. If you want me to take you outside, please just wait until I know I can heal you without holding back, when my abilities haven't all been spent on building."

Zellendine did understand that, although she didn't want to. She wanted to go outside. She needed to set foot on the planet, to feel dirt between her toes, to know what her new world looked like.

More than all that, she needed to not be stuck in a big metal and concrete tube with only shades of grey to look at all day.

But no matter what she needed, Troylus needed her to wait, and their child, ready to come in a few weeks, needed her to be okay. So she nodded and he turned her around, careful to not upset her still tenuous balance, and kissed her, his hands on either side of her face and hers resting on his chest.

He put his forehead to hers and left their makeshift room, leaving her alone, again.

Xander was able to go outside, but he rarely did, preferring to stay behind to keep an eye on her and Maurice, and another member of the crew, Mason, wasn't able to go outside because they had the same markers in their DNA as she did.

But everyone else spent their time above the spindle, building a burgh she didn't intend to live in. Part of her wanted to be out there with them if for no other reason than to get some idea of what it would be like to live in one.

She rubbed her eyes and yawned, trying not to lay back down on the bed still warm from them together and take a nap.

There didn't seem to be enough hours in the day to sleep the amount she wanted to lately. It didn't help that her feet still didn't want to move the way she needed them to, and by the end of the day she was shuffling more than walking. But every day her legs got stronger, every day her muscles were less sore and exhausted when Troylus rubbed them at night.

No matter how long the path to healing was going to be, she would see it through. And maybe, just maybe, while her brain was reconnecting things and forming new pathways around the areas that were injured, she would remember what she needed to in order to take down the Chapter.

Leaving, which is what their plan still was, felt wrong if she couldn't protect the rest of the fleet and their own people from the Chapter computers.

Once it went out into the universe, leadership would see, and they would change. She had to hang onto that belief.

Maurice's room was quiet, but the sound of gentle and rhythmic movement filtered through the blanket door.

She shoved it aside and watched while Xander finished up another round of physical therapy with their poor sleeping friend.

"How is he this time?" she asked, going to Maurice's side and picking up the holo next to him, tapping at the scan they always ran during the exercises. Nothing.

"Not even a blip?" Xander asked, catching his breath with his hands on his hips.

Zellendine shook her head, it was always the same answer, and what she wouldn't have given for it to change.

Reaching up to the tiny machine hanging on the crate at the head of Maurice's bed, she checked that it had the correct dosage settings and was plenty full. They didn't want him starving to death while they fumbled around trying to find an answer.

"We need to come up with a new idea," Xander said, bending forward and resting on his hands braced on the bottom of the bed.

"I know." She patted Maurice's hand, letting her fingers rest on his and closing her eyes on the wish that he would just wake up.

"And I don't mean for you and Troylus to make out while he's fully charged again." Xander shook his head and Zellendine smiled.

"It was worth a shot. It worked on the ship," she said and laughed as he stood up and his eyes went wide.

No, it hadn't worked this time, in fact it was a disaster that broke every makeshift wall in the main room and meant hours for everyone putting them back up, but it was worth a try. Even if it left Xander acting permanently scarred.

"Okay, so what's your idea?" she asked, following Xander out of the room and toward the medic alcove, his pace slowed so she could keep up.

"What makes you think I have an idea?"

His question was delivered serious enough, but she saw the corner of his mouth flirting with a smile.

"Because you probably wouldn't have mentioned needing to come up with something while remaining so jovial if you didn't." It was her turn to smile when he turned to face her completely and his steps stopped.

She passed him and a second later he had joined her again.

"I somehow missed the day you figured me out and, to be honest, I'm not sure how I feel about it," he said and she laughed until he joined her.

When they reached the medic alcove, she was tired, and pulled out the stool Troylus had made for her to keep tucked away for just that reason.

"Alright, go ahead, tell me your idea of how to rescue Maurice from the clutches of sleep."

40

TROYLUS

"That's the stupidest idea I've ever heard," Troylus said, "There is no fucking way."

"It's not stupid, and it might work," Imogene said, standing next to him with her arms crossed over her chest, her head cocked to the side, and a finger playing with her bottom lip, while she stared at the woods in front of them.

"We can get the ore, it's already right in the ground, we don't need to reinvent the house right now." He shook his head and looked over his shoulder at where the crew was putting the last touches on the second to last building they were required to put together before the Wheel sent more people down to settle.

"But it would be good, wouldn't it? If we could make it work and then lots of people without abilities could still build their own homes," she said, a smile on her face.

"Corto doesn't know what he's talking about," he said, rolling his eyes, and quickly losing patience because Zellendine was due any day and he wanted his dad and Indigo around to meet the baby. "Between you and I, we can get the ore out after a quick scan and shape it with no problem."

"Troylus, think." She turned to him, her eyes bright and her normally stoic face alight. "You could do this when you and Zellendine move into the mountains."

He paused with his mouth partially open and closed it as he looked from her to the forest in front of him.

"Okay," he said, and she grinned. "This is just a test. We see if it works, if it doesn't let rain in, and we call it good. If it doesn't work, we redo it right. And damn I hope that we get this done fast and it works."

"Good. Now tell me why they aren't sending a spindle down right away since we have plenty of room to house everyone." She headed toward the woods and started examining the trees. For what, he wasn't sure.

"I don't know why they aren't. At the other spindle, when I was leaving, we almost had all the building done and they were already sending the first influx of people to us. Why they want to make it more complicated for this region now, I can't tell you."

He walked along beside her as she touched the trees and poked at them. He looked around to see if anyone else was going to come near them, if he should cover for her, or pretend it was totally normal.

"Do you think it was because of the accident last time?" she asked, knocking on the trunk of one of the trees with the weird not leaves and nodding her head.

"Probably, but if they're going to do it, and listen to what we suggested, why wait? I swear, leadership's decisions will never make any sense to me."

She stepped back from the tree and smiled.

"This one," she said.

"Are you sure? Do you need to interview it first?" he asked.

"Very funny," she said, but her smile didn't slip as she raised her hands. Before he got his into place with her, though, she dropped them again, the smile falling from her face.

"Imogene, I was kidding. If you think this is the right one, then let's do it."

"What are the chances that leadership is delaying this drop off because of you?" she asked, and his stomach dropped into his feet.

He didn't know how to answer that, it left him standing there with the small amount of ability he had in him at the moment itching to get out to do this small work, and every alarm in his body going off.

"But why would they do anything because of me?" His voice was hushed and dangerous, edged with a tinge of fear and fury, all of it full of an urge to rip into leadership to protect his family. The one still on the Wheel, waiting to be allowed to step foot on the planet, and the one waiting inside the spindle buried in the clearing behind him.

"Think about it. They hate it when someone subverts their authority, messes with their plans. You and Zellendine have done so much to upend their rules over and over again. You shouldn't even be here. You were assigned to a different spindle and you stole their medic in the process of your trip through the wilderness."

Of all the things rolling through his head recently, none of it came close to being as paranoid, as suspicious, or probably as accurate as her theory.

He bit his lip and took a step toward the door to the inside, shook his head and took a step back to his place next to her. His feet shuffled, his body torn between running to Zellendine and the comms and doing something foolish, to staying and finishing his work so they would be out of excuses.

"Calm down." Imogene's face was back to her mask and her voice was an order, not a suggestion.

"Going to the comms and making an ass of yourself isn't going to help it. Telling Zellendine won't do anything but make her stressed out, which she is enough already and doesn't need. You need to file it away as one more thing to think about when you think about leadership, and get back to work."

The clear directive and logic in her statement calmed the frayed edges of his nerves just enough for him to breathe calmly and slow his heart back down to a manageable level.

He nodded and she did too, turning back to the forest and raising her hands.

"Ready?" she asked, waiting until he was in position.

Imogene's yellow light shot out of her hands, his blue right behind it, a quick burst was all they had, but it was enough to fell the tree and slice into thin shreds.

He panted and bent over, bracing himself with his hands on his knees and she collapsed to sitting next to him.

Sweat, instantly heavy on his brow, cooled in the breeze that floated through the burgh.

"Fuck, I'm glad we're almost done," he said.

The laugh she managed was short and almost a cough, but in it he heard his own thought echoed.

Other members of the crew came to them as they settled in to sit on the ground and rest. All of them listened as Imogene and Corto explained their plan, showing them how to cut the slices they had created into smaller chunks and how they should layer them so that, in theory, they acted like a leaf and water would pour off them.

People glanced at each other, some with their skepticism plain on their faces, but everyone did as they were instructed.

For Troylus, his part was done, his exhausting, and only really possible in the time they had managed to complete it in because he wasn't alone, part of the building of the burgh was done.

"Have you decided which house will be yours?" he asked, leaning back on his hands, watching closely as the last, strange house with the wooden roof was built in the second burgh he had been a part of.

"Yeah," she said, a smile on her face that she turned toward the sun, setting behind the trees and casting long shadows along the ground, "I think I'm going to live in the one least like the Wheel."

Leaning forward, he paid more attention to the details, the terrestrialness of it, how clean and new it was and how it would age like the trees and the lands around them, organically.

"Wow," he said, his own smile growing to match hers.

41

ZELLENDINE

"Wow," she said, not able to come up with any other word for Xander's untethered idea.

"I'm not sure what that response means." He looked at her with a furrowed brow and guarded eyes.

"Not really sure how to respond to be honest." She rubbed at her face, just imagining the reaction that Troylus, Imogene, and Corto would have.

"Do you think it might work?"

She shook her hands out to the side, looking for a way to explain all the things running through her head, none of which were that it might work.

"Corto is going to lose his shit, to say nothing of the others," she said, still blinking away the fact that he truly seemed to think everyone would agree to try it.

"But this could work. Think about it. The purple caused this in Maurice."

She narrowed her eyes at him and he shrugged.

"Okay, so the injuries from the purple caused this. We know it probably wasn't

Imogene because she's treated him again and nothing. Troylus has tried too. Nothing. So maybe if we go to the source, we can get the effects reversed."

"You're suggesting we take Maurice outside, in what? Our arms? And put him on the ground like bait for the purple?" Of all the stupid ass things he could have said, she couldn't get her head around this one.

"Maybe we use your chair. And he wouldn't be the bait. It wouldn't come for him according to your scans." He bit his lip and looked at the wall instead of her face.

It took her a minute, a full minute, of staring at him while he avoided her gaze and running through what he said, for her to trip and fall over the word bait. Then she crash landed on the word *him* in the sentence, it wouldn't come for him.

She almost fell off her stool and caught herself on the wall of the alcove next to her, gulping down air.

"You want to use me as bait."

He glanced at her and grimaced before he whirled around and put his hands on the top of his head while he paced.

"Troylus is going to kill me for even suggesting it," he said, not to her, but to the air as he wandered.

And he wasn't wrong.

"Oh, you think?" she asked, barely suppressing a hysterical laugh building within her.

"I thought you wanted to go out there?" he asked, turning around and facing her.

"Yeah, I do, but not as bait to a murderous space anomaly that followed me to the damn planet because it wants me dead so bad." She threw her hands into the air, how did he not see that his plan was homicidal?

"But what's the difference between this and whatever you were planning on doing out there?" he yelled.

"The difference is that Troylus couldn't even protect me in

your scenario. If he did, the thing wouldn't attack," she yelled back, standing from the stool even though she had to brace herself on the wall to do it.

"He could be right there." His hand flung out, coming close enough to her face to cause a wind that ruffled her hair.

"First of all!" She was screaming now, and she didn't care. "Watch your hands, you almost hit me in the face!"

"Oh, calm down." His voice was dismissive and he took a step back from her but she followed, narrowing the gap between them.

"Second," she screamed, not growing quiet to suit his fragile sense of calm, "You want to send me out there with nothing to protect me but a man unable to get out of a REM cycle, and stuck in a chair, when that thing shows up to kill me."

"What the fuck?" Troylus asked from behind her.

"Good, Troylus, Zellendine needs to calm down. It isn't good for the baby," Xander said.

"Fuck you," she yelled.

"Terrible fucking idea," Troylus mumbled, raising his hands in the air with his palms out like he had when they were in their room, but this time he looked genuinely horrified and scared.

"Your *friend* here," she said, gesturing at Xander, "Wants me to play bait for the purple so it can attack Maurice and in upside down land that's supposed to cure Maurice."

"Are you out of your damn mind?" Troylus yelled, advancing on Xander until Imogene grabbed him and pulled him back while he wrestled to get closer.

"No." Xander yelled back, throwing his hands around again, but being more careful not to come close to smacking anyone in the face.

Zellendine narrowed her eyes and bared her teeth, while other people around them froze and Imogene tripped Troylus who only grew more incensed.

"Someone had to say it. Maybe the purple could cure Maurice. None of us have come up with a way to do it."

"Everybody stop it," Imogene said, shoving her hands out to push Xander back and gesturing with her head to Corto who got in front of Troylus and Imogene just held a hand out toward Zellendine.

"Xander, your idea would be good except that you don't know shit about this thing. It won't just send some light at Zellendine that she can throw Maurice in front of. That's not how this damn thing works. It will turn its light into solid objects that will tear through anything in their path. Your idea would kill them both."

He opened his mouth, closed it again, and left it hanging open, his eyes growing larger by the second as his gaze moved from Imogene in front of him to Zellendine and he winced.

Xander sat down, his legs giving out beneath him, with a thump that sounded to Zellendine like it hurt.

"Do you get it now?" Imogene asked, and Xander nodded, a tear falling down his cheek.

"Your idea, and your unwillingness to listen to me, to dismiss everything I said, would have ended in death." Zellendine turned, trailing a hand along Troylus's shoulders as she headed to her room. A nap was a good idea after all.

"Some medic," Troylus said behind her and she winced for Xander.

If he was half the medic her father was, and she thought he wanted to be, Troylus's words would play in his mind forever. Maybe he would at least remember hers too. Maybe next time someone told him about an injury, or some theory of his, he would fucking listen.

She made it to her room and collapsed onto the bed, any remaining energy she had was left out in the main room dumped on Xander with her rage.

Troylus caught up to her seconds later and wrapped her in his arms.

"I got you. Nothing is going to hurt you," he said into her hair.

But she knew that wasn't true. As much as she wanted it to be, and as much as he wanted to be able to ensure that, it would never be true.

And she needed to find a way to defeat the purple, and save Maurice. It was the only way she was going to be able to come close to being as safe as she was at that moment, folded in Troylus's arms.

42

BRIAR

THE PLANET WAS STRANGELY UNIFORM FROM HERE. FAR ABOVE the world, it was all green, but he knew there were spindles and burghs down there. He knew from his days in the terraforming department that it had large differences in biodiversity from one region to another, and that there were whole sections they weren't planning to colonize at all because they were more inhospitable than others.

But from so far away, the shades of the green down below, that he could only picture in his mind, all melded into one, general color.

The strange thing weren't the spots of blue, or brown. Even the black and white spots were to be expected, but it was the purple and the pink that would appear and disappear again in flashes of brilliance that he didn't understand.

His old department must have been so busy running through the information pouring into it from all the spindles, it made him want to be back at work, buried in figures and theories.

Although anything would have been better than waiting for the medic in front of him to stop talking about the ways in which a good Chapter citizen acted and thought, and how he wasn't it.

Damn medics, all of them were as suspect as she was. They didn't know anything about him, about the ways in which he was a better citizen than they would ever be.

But Grandpa Kason knew, and he still betrayed him.

Across the large room, the old man was saying goodbye to his granddaughter, her partner, and a baby with strange golden eyes.

Every time he stole a look their way, while the medic focused on the holo in front of them that probably held a script for them to read from, the baby was staring back at him.

It didn't matter that they were all the way across the room, and he shouldn't have been able to make out much about the baby's eye color. The gold of them shone, bright and intense, especially for someone so young.

Briar wondered which burgh they would be assigned to and hoped it wasn't the same one as his family. Rhea, his little sister, would have found those eyes... What was the word she used to describe his as they turned silver? Unnerving.

"Do you have any questions?" the medic asked.

He turned back to face the small man, who shrank and swallowed in response.

"Yes," he said, "When do I get to have reports from my old department?"

The small medic twisted his mouth to the side and glanced down at his holo, tapping at it, his fingers growing more and more frantic.

"I..." He said, swallowing again, his throat bobbing, "I will have to check on that. This says you should be focused solely on recovering your good citizenship status and preparing yourself for returning to your family."

"When you give your report to leadership, let them know that it only makes sense for me to get back to my assignment in the terraforming department to get back to being a good citizen."

Eyes wide, the small man nodded.

"Good," Briar said, standing.

"But, but, but," the man stammered.

"Are we not done yet?" Briar asked, trying for condescending and landing somewhere closer to menacing. He sighed and sat back down, but turned away while the medic's voice droned on, to stare out the window again.

Passing between the Wheel and the planet, a purple ball of light traveled, stopping and turning toward the ship.

No, toward the window he was watching it through.

All the hairs on his arms stood on end.

It may have been a ball of light, but there was far more to it, he felt it watching him, studying him.

Rhea had no idea what unnerving was, this was unnerving.

Every other sound around him dropped further into the background, so insignificant to be rendered equivalent to silence.

The thing out the window, holding still and moving just enough to keep pace with the spinning of the ship, seemed to reach out to him.

He felt it, running through him, although none of the thing's light penetrated the window.

In his mind, images flashed, images he couldn't make sense of, images that ran so fast they turned into a blur.

By the time it stopped, and darted away as if nothing at all had happened, he felt dizzy.

His brain was trying to take single pieces of the images he

was given and focus on them, trying to understand the message, and a tear trickled down his cheek.

Lifting a hand to touch it, he wiped it away in a slowed and awed movement.

Dropping his hand into his lap, he looked down on a fingertip dipped in blood.

43

ZELLENDINE

"I HAVE AN IDEA," SHE SAID, SITTING AT THE TABLE AS EVERYONE turned her way, most not even taking a pause in shoveling food into their mouths.

"Okay, does it include trying to get Troylus to make that desert of his dad's again, because that's all I care about," Corto said with a grin as Troylus shook his head.

"There is more to the universe than your stomach," Imogene said, sticking her tongue out at him.

Corto put a hand to his chest and slumped to the side like he was wounded, and the other crew members smiled and focused back on their own conversations.

"What's your idea?" Troylus asked, putting a hand on hers.

"So," she said, wiggling in her seat to turn toward Troylus, her belly touching the edge of the table even as she felt too far from it, "I've been looking through the old equipment in the medic bay, hoping that maybe something in there would be helpful, and I think I found something."

"How have you had time to do that when you've been

running everyone's scans from the other regions?" Imogene asked, narrowing her eyes and looking too closely at Zellendine.

There were dark circles forming under her eyes, and she was too thin for someone growing a baby. She looked sick, she knew that, but there was this clock ticking in the back of her mind, that she needed to get Maurice cured, and do it right now, that she couldn't explain.

"I've got it all handled," she said, waving a hand. There was only so long she could run through the scans and make lists of who was safe to go outside and who wasn't before her eyes started to glaze over.

"But this is important. Maurice needs me to keep looking."

Xander was part way down the side of the table opposite Troylus and he dropped his head further toward his food.

An apology would have been nice, but he had chosen to focus solely on being the best, most attentive medic to Maurice and avoid everyone else.

"What if we're wrong, though?" Troylus asked, wrapping his hand over hers, his voice soft.

"I'm not sure what you think we're wrong about." She put heavy emphasis on the word we're, because the way he said it she thought he meant she was wrong.

"The signals in the blood, what if Maurice wasn't actually safe from the purple, and neither are all the others whose blood looks like his." Troylus's voice was still soft and his eyes softer as he tucked a stray piece of her hair behind her ear.

But she wasn't wrong. She could see that most people were like Xander and Maurice, their blood showing markers that put them somewhere between Troylus and her. Most people didn't have any signs at all suggesting they would never develop abilities. And yes, it was a theory, but it was a good one. That only people like her, who had blood and DNA that for whatever reason meant abilities couldn't live there, were the ones targeted by the purple.

"I'm not wrong, and even if I was, that doesn't mean I shouldn't keep looking for a way to wake him up." She squeezed Troylus's hand, but the corners of his mouth turned down anyway.

"Zellendine," Imogene said. "He means that it isn't your fault Maurice is hurt, you don't have to kill yourself. Other people are looking for a way to help him too."

Her words hit in quick succession the part of her that didn't want to look at the ways in which it was her fault.

She bit her lip and nodded, saying, "I know."

But the looks she got from Imogene, Troylus, even Corto, all said that they didn't believe her.

"Alright," Imogene said, pretending to move past it like Zellendine was. "Tell us this idea of yours."

"Okay," she said, taking a deep breath and shoving her guilt to the back of her mind. "So there's this thing, it has instructions with it, and I guess it works pretty well, because there's a ton of documentation with it, notes and things about the times it was used. But anyway, this thing uses electric pulses to restart the heart."

She popped a bite of food in her mouth, smiling around it while they all froze. It was brilliant, she knew it was going to work. They must have thought the same thing. It was sitting there all this time.

"Zellendine, that could kill him," Corto said, his face reanimating and turning from shock to horror.

"No, no, it won't. It isn't high enough to electrocute him, but it's just strong enough to make your heart skip and restart, and isn't that what we need to happen, for him to restart?"

"He's not a holo that is malfunctioning," Imogene said, shaking her head.

"Come on, that's not what I meant."

Everyone started talking at the same time, the general consensus that she was very wrong and it was the worst idea she had ever had.

She sat at the table and let them talk, knowing she was right and they just didn't understand. Her head was cocked to the side and she ate bite after bite, tuning them out and staring at her plate.

When she looked up, she caught Xander looking at her, his face not the dejected one he had been wearing for the last couple days.

He kept eye contact with her and tipped his head, a nod before he turned away and got up from the table, dropping his plate off in the service and walking away.

"I know you want to help him any way you can, but this isn't it," Troylus said, giving her a kiss on her hand. "Maybe it would be best if you would take a day to rest a little bit, I don't want you to run yourself down." He put a hand to her cheek and she leaned into it, even though he was wrong, he was loving.

"The only way for me to not be run down would be to give birth, and I have no control over that." She smiled and kissed his palm, him returning her smile.

"Any time, little one," he said, putting a hand to her stomach.

"Have you two picked a name yet?" Corto asked, grabbing another bar from the middle of the table even though he had eaten more than most of them ate all day already.

She grinned and looked to Troylus.

"No. She's being difficult."

"Hey, I don't think it's difficult to know what I want to name the baby." Her grin was massive as people started to ask and to guess.

"But what you want to name the baby is not a name," he said, laughing and rubbing the back of his neck.

"What's the name?" Corto asked, chewing with a smile on his face.

He was very invested, and looking around the table, everyone was listening intently, most of them smiling.

"River," she said.

"That's a great name," Imogene said as Corto choked on a bite of his food.

"You don't think so?" she asked him, trying and failing to suppress her laugh as Imogene pounded him on the back and he finally got it under control.

"No," he croaked, his voice not right yet, "It's fine."

"See?" Troylus gestured to Corto. "It's not a name."

"My name starts with a Z and I'm pretty sure my parents were just putting sounds together." She shook her head when he tried to hide his smile.

"Will other kids tease ours over their name?" he asked, his eyes wide and she patted his hand.

"Are you feeling really guilty about all the grief you gave me when we were little?" She smiled and batted her eyelashes at him while it was Imogene's turn to choke on laughter.

"You're worried other kids will be jerks because you were?" She leaned into Corto and laughed until tears were coming out of her eyes.

"That's not funny, Imogene." Troylus had one eyebrow high.

"I mean," Zellendine said, turning aside to hide her smile, "It's kind of funny."

"We're all doomed to worry that our kids will be exactly like us, and that all other kids will be exactly like us to our kid," Corto said, shaking his head.

Zellendine cocked her head to the side and the laughter stopped. Of all the people to be philosophical and bring wisdom to the conversation, she never would have thought it would be Corto. But it made her appreciate him more.

"That's very wise, Corto," she said.

He pulled his head back, his eyes going wide and his mouth turning into a thin line.

"I don't know if I want to be called wise. That's a lot to live up t—"

A crash, a pop, and a fizzle sound cut him off.

She turned, as everyone else did, toward the sound in the middle of the main room, looking for what the source was.

From near the makeshift rooms, a puff of smoke wafted up toward the ceiling high above.

44

TROYLUS

"What in the universe," Troylus muttered, jumping up from the table and running to where he thought the smoke came from.

Imogene was on his heels, with Corto and others. Zellendine trailed behind them all, her walk more a waddle now, but at least she shuffled her feet less. She was getting stronger all the time.

"Hey," he said, weaving through makeshift walls, trying to find the right place. "Are you okay?"

Troylus wasn't even sure who he was talking to, probably Xander, but maybe someone else had slipped from the table while they were laughing about names and he missed it.

Rounding a corner, the smell of burnt hair floated by and he made a turn toward it. One more turn brought him to the what was the front of Maurice's room.

"Fuck, somebody help," he yelled, kicking the thing in Xander's hand with flames engulfing it away. He grabbed onto his not burned hand and dragged him away from the edge of the blanket wall on the side. The piece over the door was wrapped around his upper body like he was wearing it, and the pole holding it up was broken and off to one side.

Others ran over and helped him put out the flames while Zellendine made her way through the crowd to Xander's side, checking him with careful fingers and practiced, calm movements.

"He's okay," she said, and not a second later Xander stirred, just enough to moan and thrash from side to side.

"Someone go check on Maurice." She looked up at Troylus and gestured with her head.

Nodding, and turning around, he went into the room to find Maurice sitting up in the bed, his uniform open in the front and his eyes blinking as he sucked in giant breaths and his hands shook.

"Maurice?" Troylus asked, his voice low and gentle like he would use when speaking to a yawx.

"I…" He looked down at his own shaking hands, and tucked them under his arms, hugging himself. "Troylus, how are you here? What happened?"

"Oh, universe," Zellendine said behind him, darting past him to run to Maurice and sit on the edge of the bed. "Hey. I'm so glad you're awake."

She ran through the same checks as she had on Xander while Maurice stared with wide eyes at her belly.

"Zellendine, how did you get so big?" he asked, smiling down at her and reaching a hand out like he was going to touch her but curling his fingers back in at the last second.

"We have a lot to tell you," she said.

Troylus left her to catch Maurice up on how much, exactly, he had missed. It wasn't a conversation he felt prepared to help his friend through, that first realization. The aftermath? Sure. But that first stark moment when he learned he had missed months? That was better left to his professional medic partner.

But how in the universe did Maurice wake up?

He shook his head as he peeked through bodies to where Xander was sitting up, supported by Imogene and Corto.

"Is he okay?" Xander asked, although his tongue sounded thick.

"Who?" Corto asked, looking around like they had missed someone else laying on the floor on fire.

"Maurice is fine. Zellendine is checking him now," Troylus said, and people moved so he could crouch down in front of Xander whose mouth twitched like he was trying to smile but couldn't quite remember how.

"Tell her it worked," he said, and closed his eyes as a real smile bloomed on his face.

"What worked?" Corto asked, handing Xander off to Mason and other people who were talking about taking him back to his room and getting him some water.

"I..." Troylus looked back toward the room where Zellendine was with Maurice, going over all he had lost, and having no idea that it was her untethered idea that brought him back and made sure he wouldn't miss anymore. "I think he means that thing," he pointed to the thing with the cords hanging off it, one of them charred and melted, "was part of Zellendine's idea and it woke up Maurice."

His words were like the purple had just showed up, everyone started talking at once. The stream of crew going in to check on Maurice was constant while others asked him questions he didn't have the answers to. And more returned to talk excitedly amongst themselves about her, her idea, and the rare comet that they were all witnesses to.

Troylus just stood to the side, his mind filled with her, while he shook his head and smiled.

Finally, the pandemonium died down, Corto and Imogene

helped Maurice from the room on shaky legs to get something to eat and a good wash.

He waited until they had passed him to go into the room, just as Zellendine levered herself up from the bed.

She smiled up at him, and the pallor of too thin and too stressed, just at the edge of sick and injured she had worn since he came to her spindle fell away. Instead, she looked like a distant star, shining, radiant, and it left him in awe.

"You did it," he said, and she closed her eyes for a second like she was relishing in the relief of it working.

Troylus reached up to run a hand along her cheek.

"Your absolutely untethered idea born of exhaustion." He kissed her other cheek. "Running yourself ragged." He ran his other hand down her arm to link his fingers with hers. "And your inability to stop when you think you need to do something."

He leaned down and kissed her on the lips as she wrapped her arms around his neck and sighed.

"Speaking of stopping," she said, with a yawn so large her jaw popped, "You need to get out there and finish that last house so we can get everyone home and stop working so damn hard. They said yesterday, as soon as they got word it was finished they would all come down."

"Okay, but how about I put you to bed so you can take a nap."

Zellendine smiled and he walked her to their room, tucking her in and kissing her on the forehead before he left the spindle to finish what he started.

Troylus looked at the pile of wood chunks left to attach, it would take the crew all day, or he could try and do it with his ability. Part of him wanted to work on it without any light involved, even if it was only to finish it all out. But he wanted to get on the comms.

He smiled and raised his hands, but purple light danced in front of him, swirling around and in on itself like it was examining the area.

Before he could think about it, he took a step backward toward the door, but froze when the purple swirled closer to him in a flash.

"What are you?" he asked, his voice hushed and smaller than he wanted it to be.

The light stopped swirling, instead it just held steady, the edges fluctuating.

A hum rose from the trees and the light shot into the air, disappearing into the blue, causing pink streaks to form.

He sucked in a deep breath, the yawx peeking eyes between the branches.

"Thank you," he said.

It didn't matter that he knew the light wasn't going to hurt him, it would kill Zellendine the first chance it got, and it scared the living shit out of him.

No way was he going to have everyone outside working all day, remaining vulnerable to it while it floated through air looking benign.

He raised his hands and shoved all the fear he felt facing something as innocuous seeming as a light and forced it out to the pieces and the last house.

They darted through the air, their movements not floating or careful. Direct shots from the ground in their neat stacks to their places on the roof, their fixtures driving home, and the last pieces of structure slamming into place.

By the time the last one popped into place his blue light was thin and tinged through with the colors on the other side of it like they were stronger than his ability.

Maybe the reality on the ground was stronger than his ability.

He sat down, hard, and tried to measure if his light was still lessening, or if it had leveled off. It didn't matter, his work on the burghs was done. If he still had enough to build a house for Zellendine and the baby in the woods when they figured out how to defend from the purple, he would call it a bonus and not miss having it when it was gone.

Of all the buildings in the burgh, he liked the curved roof with its layered pieces of wood in the one he just finished. Maybe he would build them a house just like it.

Laying on the ground, soaking in the heat of the sun's rays, he watched as the pink ran across the sky and amended his wishes. If the only thing that kept Zellendine safe from the purple was his ability, he never wanted it to leave him.

45

ZELLENDINE

She woke up to a sharp stab that ran across her belly like a cramp that didn't let go, it just grew and grew.

It didn't matter that she knew she needed to breathe, catching her breath was impossible.

Until it stopped.

Dragging air in and out, she swung her legs over the edge of the bed and grabbed the jar Imogene had made for her for just that moment.

Shaking the jar as hard as she could, the couple things inside rattled against the sides with a screaming ring, their sound painful to her own ears and hopefully loud enough for everyone to hear it.

Pushing off from the bed, she managed to stand with a hand on the small of her back.

Walking, although not at all what she felt like doing, was the best thing for her at the moment.

Troylus was outside.

She sent him outside.

She squeezed her eyes shut, hoping he would get back to her

soon, and hoping someone had already sent the comm so Rullon and Indigo would be on their way soon.

On the occasions she thought about having a child when she was young, it involved a mechanical womb, a scheduled moment, and nothing but the celebration without any of the pain or work she was about to experience.

It didn't matter that the holo, her training, even her father, all made it sound like something that she shouldn't be afraid of, deep in her bones there was so little that wasn't shaking, she wanted someone to punch her hard enough to knock her out so she could wake up when it was done.

Mason was the first to arrive, whipping the blanket door back, eyebrows high, eyes wide.

Zellendine nodded as she paced.

"I'll get Troylus," Mason said, dropping the blanket and running, the sound of feet squeaking followed them.

"Okay, Troylus is coming." She rubbed her belly and continued pacing, her steps steady and regular even though she still had to focus more than she did before on making them that way, they were greatly improved.

"Are you still sleeping?" Corto asked on the other side of the blanket, his voice quiet.

"No," she said, almost laughing, "I'm not asleep."

"Listen." He shoved the blanket aside and stood there chewing on his lip while she kept pacing, wondering if he was going to offer to help with the birth. "I did something and I just want to know if you think Troylus will be mad that he didn't get to do it."

"What did you do?" And why was this important right now?

"I sent a comm saying we were done with building and to send the spindle."

"Troylus will be thrilled, when did you send it?" Her steps

stuttered, but she kept pacing, waiting for the next wave of contractions.

"Yesterday, as soon as we got to the last building," he said, his face scrunched up like he had cooked a meal he thought she wouldn't like.

"Corto, it's great, honestly. Oh," she said, stopping all words and her walking when another wave wrapped around her middle and spread to grip her entire body from her breasts to her knees in the same pain.

"Zellendine?" he asked, knowledge slowly dawning on his face until he was standing just beyond her doorway with his hands hanging limply at his sides, and his mouth wide open.

Finally, it stopped, and she could take whole and pain free breaths again, she looked at Corto who was a strange color around the eyes.

"Are you okay?" she asked as she started pacing again.

"You… You… You're having a baby," he stammered.

She laughed and looked down at her large belly, managing not to say, you think?

"I… I… I… I'll go get Xander," he said, turning without changing the look on his face.

"No, Corto, not Xander. Get Imogene."

He nodded and turned in the other direction, walking off as if he still wasn't seeing correctly.

On her own again, she wanted to sit down, lay down, anything but pace more, but that wasn't going to happen. So, pacing was the plan.

The tiny room, five steps one way, turn, and five steps the other way, left her feeling dizzy.

Where was Imogene? Where was Troylus?

Her back ached and it felt like in a matter of minutes her belly was lower, pulling on her back in a way it wasn't earlier that day.

"You okay?" Imogene's calm voice was like a wash on her fraying nerves.

"Thank the universe you're here. It's time," she said and Imogene just nodded.

She got to Zellendine's side and walked with her out of the room to pace up and down in front of it instead.

"Out here we can go farther before we have to turn around. You just stop when you need to." Imogene kept one hand on Zellendine's back, making circles with her palm.

Zellendine smiled and took a deep breath. She wasn't alone, and no matter what happened next, that wouldn't change.

"Did you get all the information you think you'll need? Are you sure you're ready for this?" she asked Imogene, watching her face for any hint of doubt, but of course there was none. Her silver eyes gave nothing away if she didn't want them to.

"Yes. Now stop worrying about me. Mason will bring all the bags you've packed with the supplies, and if we need to, get a wash ready." Imogene smiled, but it didn't reach her eyes, it was just a flash of reassurance.

She nodded and stopped, the wave back and stronger than before.

By the time it stopped, she was gasping and her knees shook, sweat had popped out on her forehead.

"Can I do this, Imogene? Tell me I can do this."

"You can do this. You learned to walk again, you recovered from something that would have killed most people. This is nothing. By tomorrow you'll have River in your arms, and this won't bother you at all." Imogene nodded and they started walking again while Zellendine repeated the words in her head.

They turned at the end of the row of makeshift rooms and Troylus rounded the other end at a sprint, almost losing his footing.

He slammed to a halt when he saw her, taking a deep breath as a smile bloomed on his face.

Zellendine smiled back and felt something release and heard a weird little pop.

Liquid poured down her legs and splashed onto the floor.

"Oh," she said.

It really was time.

4 6

TROYLUS

THERE WAS NO WAY THIS WAS HOW IT WAS SUPPOSED TO BE, something had to be catastrophically wrong.

"Zellendine, please, let Xander help," he begged, putting his forehead to the back of her hand, bent over the edge of the bed like her supplicant.

Which, as far as he was concerned, wasn't that far off from reality, and he would have been happy to worship her every minute of every day, if she just survived.

She turned her head, her eyes not quite focused on his, sweat heavy on her brow and her breaths too shallow.

But she smiled and said, "No. Imogene and Mason can help me, this is normal. I'm fine."

He might have believed her if her fine hadn't been clipped short by a grunt as she curled forward over her rounded belly that rolled and moved on its own in ways he didn't understand.

"Imogene," he said, not sure what else he could have added that he hadn't already said, but damn it he had to think of something. Zellendine couldn't go on like this.

"Just stop whining, and brace her back," Imogene said,

tapping a holo and studying whatever she found there with Mason.

"No birthing on the ship was ever like this," he said, reaching around Zellendine's back to support her while she gritted her teeth and breathed in giant, heaving breaths, in and out, in a careful rhythm she only broke when she laid back again. It was wave after wave of slowly watching her die.

"Come on, Imogene, Mason, do something," he begged.

"According to her, and the files she's showed us," Mason said, their voice careful and calm enough to make Troylus want to punch them, "This is normal, and the birthings on the ship were done by machines that none of us could see inside of."

Zellendine squeezed his hand still in hers so tight his finger bones ground together, then she collapsed back into his arm.

"What can I do?" he asked her, wiping her drenched hair from her face.

"Shut up." She smiled and grimaced, folding over on herself again.

"It's happening faster, giving her less time in between." His voice had taken on the tremor he wouldn't let into his hands as he held her, but there was nothing he could do to stop it.

"Also normal," Imogene said and she didn't flinch when he looked at her even though he was sure his face betrayed his want to punch everyone.

"Not normal. The wombs didn't look like they were turning inside out." Damn it, why wasn't anyone else worried?

"The wombs are machines, she's a human, it's more compli-cated." Mason said, tapping again on the holo between them and Imogene.

"Will you two at least pay attention?" he yelled, his hold on his helpless anger beginning to fail.

She relaxed again, but didn't even lean as far back as she had before, just stopped her straining and slumped into him.

"Troylus?" she said, her voice breathy and thin.

"Yes, anything," he stammered, kissing her cheek.

"Please, don't argue anymore, or I'm going to make you wait out - " She sucked air in through her teeth before she finished, "side." And curled over again.

"Imogene," he said, his voice a plaintive whine, and he wasn't sorry anymore, not for his whining or his worry, because blood spread across the blanket from between her legs.

"Get out, Troylus." Imogene leaned over the end of the bed and lifting the altered uniform to look underneath.

"Excuse me," he said, putting a hand out to shove the fabric back over Zellendine's lower half.

"You need to go, this next part is going to make you lose your control on your ability, which I know is back by now, and I don't really want to end up swallowed by random crap." She raised a brow at him and he chewed on his lip.

"I swear, I won't throw everything at you and bury you in whatever parts of the spindle aren't permanently attached." His voice wasn't conciliatory, and he didn't mean it to be. There was no world in the universe in which he would abandon Zellendine.

"Damn it, don't be a pain in the ass. Just listen to me, you're not going to be able to handle it." Imogene said, standing and moving to grab a tray full of objects he didn't even want to think about the need for, sharp, bladed instruments, needles, bandages, even scissors.

He swallowed and cringed, putting his head against Zellendine's as a whimper escaped through her clenched teeth.

"If she can handle this, I can handle being here for her," he said, his voice low and betraying the fact he was fighting back tears.

Zellendine cried out and clutched at his hand, grinding his fingers in her own.

"You are amazing," he said, his lips moving against her cheek. "If anyone can do this, you can. It will be over soon."

He wasn't even sure if he was telling her the truth. But it didn't matter. He kept talking.

While she labored, and fought through the pain, he told her he loved her, he was sorry she hurt, that if he could make it stop hurting he would. He told her anything, anything at all.

For hours, her struggle and his words mingled in twin and opposite songs.

And she eventually turned her head toward him, tears glistening in her eyes and her face a rictus of pain, but she focused on him completely.

"Zellendine," he breathed, his forehead pressing against her hot and sweat drenched one.

She squeezed her eyes shut, clenched her teeth, and held back a scream so that it came out as a whimper. Her whole body, every muscle and sinew in it clenched up so tight she shook with the force of it.

Her eyes opened, and her body relaxed, a smile growing on her face.

Crying. He heard crying.

"The baby's here," Imogene said.

Zellendine turned, so did Troylus.

Imogene held a tiny baby, wrapped in a scrap of blanket, out to Zellendine's outstretched arms.

Fine fuzz dusted the top of the baby's head, the little cupid's bow mouth working in squawks almost as small as the baby itself.

"Oh," Zellendine said, her eyes drifting toward closed, and her breath coming in big relieved waves.

"Troylus, will you take the baby for a few minutes while Xander comes in and sees to Zellendine now?" Imogene asked, laying out additional instruments she hadn't used before.

"But why? Are you okay?" he asked, taking the baby but trying to study Zellendine's face for any sign that something was very wrong.

She smiled, but her eyes went closed again and stayed closed.

"Xander," Troylus yelled, jumping up from the edge of the bed.

He must have been waiting for the call because mere seconds later he pushed back the blanket door and stepped inside.

Troylus kissed the top of the baby's head and thrust his new child at Xander.

"What are you doing?" Xander asked, taking the baby and looking over it with a holo in hand.

"I'm finally able to help," Troylus said, sitting next to Zellendine's limp form, noting that at least she was breathing well, and putting his hands on either side of her abdomen.

Heal, he thought, pouring every bit of the will it took for him to hold his ability back for the hours she suffered into the act of making her better, of helping in the only way he could.

"Maybe you should let me do my assignment and let her heal naturally," Xander said from behind him.

But if he could make any part of the process easier on her, he would, and there was no way he was letting her continue in any kind of pain or slow, laborious getting better like she had struggled with her brain, if he could stop it. So, instead of letting up, he doubled his concentration, and his effort.

Until he fell over.

47

ZELLENDINE

She woke up and forgot for a moment where she was, her hand straying to a whole new stomach. It wasn't as flat as it had been before, the skin felt disconnected somehow, like it slipped around her body more than it should.

The feel of it reminded her that she wasn't pregnant anymore.

River. Her baby was somewhere in the spindle waiting for her.

Blinking, she sat up in a second, her heart pounding.

Swinging her legs over the side of the bed she looked around for a uniform and spotted Troylus in a chair next to the bed, the baby in his arms, and a smile on his face while he slept.

Whatever her plan had been, to go find her baby, feed him, go to the wet room, she couldn't remember anymore.

All she wanted to do was spend as many hours as they were asleep together sitting right there, watching them.

Troylus snapped his head up and looked down at the baby, his smile growing softer as he did. After he checked that the baby was still asleep he looked over to the bed and she lost herself in his silver eyes.

"Hey," he said, "How do you feel?"

"I feel fine, actually. I expected to be sore and need a lot of recuperation." She shook her head, not understanding how all the medic notes of what to expect were so wrong.

"Well, I did use some of my ability on you." He cringed. "I hope that's okay."

She had to stop the laugh bubbling up inside her, she didn't want to wake the baby, but she smiled at him and nodded. It was more than okay.

"Did you…" She looked down at the tiny bundle in his arms and suddenly her own felt empty.

"Did I what?" He grinned like he read her mind.

"I need to know what to call my baby." She almost cried, the tears pushing against the back of her eyes, but she shoved them down. He made it easier as he got up from the chair and sat next to her on the bed, passing the tiny, perfect bundle.

"Zellendine, meet River, your son." Troylus put a hand on the top of the baby's head as River yawned and wiggled before settling back into sleep. "River, meet mommy."

"Mommy," she said, the tears making their way past her blocks to keep them at bay. Her mother should have been there. Her father should have too. They should have known River, and known her as Mommy.

She bent down and kissed the top of his head, breathing in the smell of baby and making a promise to him that she would be around, she would get to see more of him growing up than her own mother had with her. The universe wasn't fair, but it owed her this, it owed River this after taking three of his grandparents.

"Yeah," Troylus said as she sat back up and looked at him, the tears only falling faster. He swept a lock of her hair away from her face and a tear away with his thumb. "I love you."

"I love you too," she said, and it had never been more true.

He kissed her, and leaned his forehead against hers, his hand still on her cheek.

"You named him a not name," she said and he smiled.

"Well, his mom is kind of amazing, and I just thought—"

She cut him off with a kiss and would have deepened it, but her stomach roared to life and it was like a cue to the rest of her body.

There was a general layer of yuck all over her, she needed a wash desperately, she was hungry and thirsty, and she really needed to pee.

"Can we maybe go to the wet room and get cleaned up before we head to food?" she asked, pulling back from him with a smile.

"Yes. We will do whatever you want." He kissed her nose and picked up the baby, in the process, the baby flung his little fists out and slammed one into her arm.

Images shot through her, leaving her shaking and grinding her teeth so she didn't scream. The power of them, the pain, the instant rise and fall of things her mind had blocked and hidden from her in the damaged parts reconnected to her accessible memories.

All of it in an instant, including discovering her father's body and the code he left her.

She grabbed at Troylus, catching his uniform and clutching it in one hand while her other hand shook where it was planted on the bed.

Tremors ran up and down her body, firing every nerve ending and causing every muscle to spasm.

"Zellendine," Troylus yelled, and the baby woke up to cry.

"What's going on?" Imogene's voice called out, but she

couldn't answer yet, she was trapped in whatever was happening in her mind.

"I don't know, she was fine. Shhh, buddy, it's okay."

River screamed, his voice bigger than his body, and finally her shaking slowed. The images started to fall into her memory instead of being in front of her.

She was left panting and more exhausted than she was when she went to take her nap the day before, leaning on her hand and not sure if she could stand.

"I remember," she said, blinking up at Imogene and Troylus as he did a strange bop and looked back and forth between the baby and her.

"You remember?" Imogene asked, her confusion plain on her face.

"Everything." She looked at Troylus as his face changed from pinched with concern to dawning realization.

"How? Just all the sudden it came back?" he asked, River finally starting to settle back to sleep.

"All at once, when…" she trailed off, looking down at the baby in his arms, one little fist in the air above him still, even in sleep.

"When what?" Imogene looked from her to Troylus and back, her face not at all the mask it sometimes was, she looked like she was about to pull her hair out.

"River was startled and smacked me."

Troylus looked down at the baby, Imogene's mask slipped into place as she stared at him too, and Zellendine smiled.

"He's like you, isn't he?" she asked, grinning up at Troylus, "Does he have silver eyes?"

"No, they're light brown. I thought he was like you," Troylus said, taking a sighing breath as tears collected in his eyes.

"More abilities. Okay, well, as long as everyone's not dying, I'm going back to bed to get ready for the big morning."

Imogene said, turning on her heel and shoving through the door, mumbling under her breath, "Too many damn big days."

"What does she mean about a big morning?" Zellendine asked, getting up from the bed on shaky legs and collecting clothes for them to change into.

"I have no idea, but we have a big night left," he said, and she raised an eyebrow at him.

"You know we don't for a while, right?" she asked, and had to stifle her laugh when his mouth dropped open.

"Of course I know that, you told me, and that's not what I meant."

She kissed him on the cheek and he followed her out of their room.

4 8

———

TROYLUS

"Are you sure we should do this now?" he asked, leaning over Zellendine's shoulder, her hair still wet from the wash, as she used the code in the comms to send a generic message about their successful terraforming.

"They'll never know to check that a fake one went through, and they'll never notice or suspect anything from what we are sending in comparison to what is normally sent. Trust me, if this bounces back we'll know I'm wrong about the code, but if I'm right, this is the perfect test." She tapped the last button and sat back.

"Done," she said.

He let out a giant breath, there was no going back now. They were tapped into the inter Chapter comms, if this worked, they had a chance to take them all down.

"Are you sure we shouldn't have waited until the morning?" he asked, biting his lip.

"It is morning." She turned around and slipped River from Troylus's arms into her own without even a flinch from his tiny face.

"How do you do that? I feel like I'm holding a sun and if I move wrong he'll go super nova, but you hold him like an extension of your body." He shook his head.

"Well, he was an extension of my body until yesterday." She laughed and bent over the comms, pushing a button and calling up the list of received messages, waiting for the confirmation.

"But, what's this?" she asked, pushing another button on the last message in the cue.

Troylus rubbed his face, the stolen moments of sleep in the last few days weren't enough. Why had no one warned him that babies didn't sleep like normal people?

She made a sound somewhere between a squeak and a squeal, her hand slamming over her mouth.

"What's wrong? Did it not go through?" he asked, leaning forward and blinking trying to force himself to make out what was before him.

"No, Troylus, the next spindle arrives this morning."

Zellendine turned around, her eyes wide and a smile taking over her face.

"My family is coming?" he asked, his voice quiet.

"Yes, they get to meet River." She took his hand in hers and turned back to the comms, one more tap on the button said their code worked.

A shiver ran through him.

"We're so close, to everything now, all we've been heading for, we're almost there," she said, and he could only nod.

"All we have to do is wait for them to arrive and send out the message."

She turned around and gave him a kiss, her face bright and showing no sign of being as tired as he was, it was like the news washed it all away for her.

"Come on, let's get some food."

He wandered after her, the other crew starting to make their way to the table, including Maurice, who walked with Corto's help, but walked, and got to the table and sat before they made it across the room to join him.

"Maurice," he said, sitting next to him and smiling when his friend turned toward him, rubbing his eyes.

"Troylus," Maurice said, clapping him on the shoulder, a touch he never would have dared to do on the Wheel.

"Damn, I'm glad you're awake." Troylus patted him on the shoulder in return, a shoulder that moved at his touch instead of lying in a bed with no reaction.

"You have no idea how happy I am about it." Maurice laughed, his voice the same as before, although Troylus wasn't sure why he expected it to be different.

Maybe because after all that time, the idea that it wouldn't leave a lasting sign was odd.

"So, who is going out to meet the spindle this morning?" Troylus asked, directing his words to the rest of the table.

A chorus of I am sounded around him and left him smiling.

Zellendine looked down at River and chewed on her lip.

"You don't have to go outside," Troylus said, putting a hand on hers.

"I want to, though." She looked up at him, her teeth working her lip.

He nodded and touched her chin, she stopped chewing.

"That's okay. I've got you. We'll be careful." He picked up her hand and kissed the back of it.

She looked back down at the baby and sighed.

"But someone else should hold River. If it comes for me, I don't want him to get hurt inadvertently like Maurice."

Furrowing his brow, Troylus scanned the people at the table, taking stock of who was staying inside and who would be meeting the spindle, and who would be the safest person for River to be with while he was protecting Zellendine.

"Imogene," he said, and she raised a brow, leaving that as her only answer, her eyes heavy.

He grimaced, "You're exhausted, never mind."

"No, it's fine." She waved it away and opened her eyes a fraction more. "What's happening?"

"Zellendine wants to see outside, and is hoping to be there to meet the spindle."

The entire table turned to look at her, most of them with their mouths open and eyes pinched.

"And you want to know if I'll hold little man so you can protect her?" Imogene asked, a few of the others relaxing in response.

"Will you?"

She rolled her eyes and smiled. "Don't be stupid."

"Good," Troylus said at the same time Zellendine said, "Thank you."

"How was that her agreeing?" Maurice asked, and Troylus couldn't help it, he laughed.

"You've missed some things, but don't worry, you'll catch up fast." Zellendine winked at him and Maurice smiled, ducking his head.

"Are you actually blushing?" Troylus asked, making Maurice turn even more red.

"Leave the man alone," Mason said, walking by with a plate piled high with food.

"Wait." Corto turned to Zellendine and Troylus, looking back and forth between them and the baby, his face falling more by the second. "Does this mean you'll be leaving us soon?"

The entire table turned to look at them, and he couldn't meet their eyes for more than a few seconds. Because the answer was yes. Their days in the spindle surrounded by the friends they were with right now, were limited.

"Don't worry, Corto," Xander said, sitting, slowly and

gingerly at the end of one bench, wincing as he settled. "They'll come back regularly to trade, and Zellendine would be the best person to help others when the first births start happening."

Xander smiled and Zellendine returned it, both of them warm and understanding, although Troylus had no idea when that had happened.

"Okay, people," Imogene said, clapping her hands together, "Eat up. We need to get out there."

4 9

BRIAR

"WHAT DO YOU MEAN?" BRIAR ASKED, HIS VOICE FLAT BECAUSE IF it wasn't he would be screaming.

"The decision has been made," Grandpa Kason said, his mouth downturned like he was oh, so sad, but his eyes were dancing and the lines at the corners were more pronounced. "All of leadership, including from the other Chapter ships, has decided that you need a longer period working through your… issues with rage."

"I am, I have been, this entire time all I do is work on it according to what you ask." He flexed his hands and curled them back into fists, it was taking so long to get through this, to listen to them bash him, the tips of his fingers were starting to go numb.

"Normally," Alara said, "we would agree, but you haven't actually been doing the work. Going through the motions isn't enough for everyone to keep moving forward."

"You're wrong." He stood up straighter, staring down his nose at them as some leaders recoiled like he had slapped them.

It made him want to. Just so they could see what it would really feel like.

She opened her mouth to speak but he barreled over her.

"Keep moving forward. That's what you say, that's how you keep all of us in line, not asking too many questions, forcing us to keep doing the work you need us to." He stepped forward, closer to them and some leaned back, they looked like they were cringing, and it brought a feral smile to his face.

"Briar, making accusations against our very way of life isn't going to help you." Grandpa Kason said.

Out of the corner of his eye, through the window, he watched as yet another spindle without him on it left the ship and headed toward the planet.

The purple formed out of the dark of space and lazily wrapped around the spindle.

It approved of the occupants.

While leadership droned on, the only communication he paid attention to was the too brief one he had experienced with the whole Grimm solar system through the purple.

He was just as the purple, a soldier for a greater good.

"I am not making accusations," he said, turning his eyes to the aged traitor in front of him. "I am speaking truths. None of you live faithfully for the Chapter. If you did, half the people on the planet would be sent out a chute."

"That's murder," Alara hissed, and someone screamed although it was stifled in an instant.

"No, that's courage." His voice was a sharp crack, and he couldn't keep his flames back anymore, with a sigh of relief and whoosh, they bloomed to life in his hands and up his arms.

"Briar, stop." Grandpa Kason jumped to his feet, abandoning all pretense of the old and infirm, but it didn't matter because the others were too busy scrambling back.

He flung out a hand and a ball of fire shot through the air, slamming into some of the people trying to get out of the gathering room.

"No." Wails, screams, and words full of hate filled the air.

"This is your leadership?"

"Running? Tripping over each other and stepping over the dead?"

Grandpa Kason slipped out the door, looking behind him, and Briar took off after him.

"Briar, please, stop," Alara yelled, from where she was crouched next to someone with burns on one arm as they screamed and writhed. Even then she didn't touch the person, following protocol.

Fire, thrown from his hand, slammed into the person and their pain stopped.

As he walked, people threw themselves out of his way.

It was easy to spot Grandpa Kason, he was too old to make his way through the still somewhat full hallways with any kind of force, and he was part of the Chapter for too long to risk touching anyone anyway.

They were all like that.

Easy. It was easy for him to burn a path through the bodies of the people between him and the old man, the only thing that slowed him down was stepping over the bodies.

"Briar, stop," Grandpa Kason screamed over his shoulder, his head swiveling back and forth between the jam of people pressing forward to get safe in front of him and Briar coming up behind him.

"No, old man. This is how it works. You did wrong, and you need to be punished."

He slammed a ball of fire into one of the cursed, the people like Zellendine who made his fire blare hotter, the ones who didn't belong.

She screamed, but it gurgled out in seconds as the fire ate

through her throat, her head toppling off and rolling along the floor toward Grandpa Kason.

The wail the old man unleashed was high pitched and piercing, his hands fluttering at his own wrinkled neck.

Passing a doorway to a room with a large window, the turning of the ship revealed an incredible view of the sun.

Its warmth was just on the other side of the glass. All he wanted was to feel it on his face. More than the pure energy, as tangible to him as water, that managed to make it through all the filters and fill him up, he wanted to experience the sun on his face and the heat on his cheeks. The things they were told they would get to one day.

"Get out of the way," Grandpa Kason yelled at the people in front of him.

Even then, Briar couldn't drown out his voice.

"Shut up." He slammed his hands together and a long trail of fire hurdled at Grandpa Kason, hammered into him and wrapped his entire body in fire.

There was no screaming, no orders, nothing from the old man after that.

Blissful silence grew in Briar's mind.

Other people in the hallway ran with their mouths open, their eyes wide. They scrambled, tripped, and tried to get anywhere but there.

And yet, Briar didn't hear any of them.

He only bothered to pay them any attention when one of them was like her. Then he put the poor, sad, unworthy out of their misery.

What he wanted was on the other side of the glass.

The room was empty. A door on the other side of the space hung open, swinging.

Out the window, the sun filled up the entire view, and his own fire snapped and swirled above his head in response.

He closed his eyes for a long moment to soak in the power of his own sun.

When he opened them again, the Wheel was starting to pass the star in its turning, leaving it behind so Briar wouldn't be able to see it anymore in mere seconds.

No spindle was ever going to get him to the planet, leadership was too far gone to see the right answers.

All he wanted was to feel the sun.

Briar raised his hands.

5 0

TROYLUS

ZELLENDINE WAS TUCKED UNDER HIS ARM, HER HAND GRIPPED onto the back of his uniform so tight it pulled the neck down enough to make it feel like he was choking.

"Please ease up a little back there," he said, his voice thin.

"Sorry," she said, her gaze roaming everywhere, while she adjusted her grab without letting go.

He rubbed his hand up and down her arm, looking to the pink streaks in the sky, waiting for the worst.

Imogene walked far in front of them, River tucked safe in her arms.

Part of him had a hard time looking at them, wanting to snatch his baby back and run into the spindle with him and Zellendine and never let the purple near them again.

But another part of him knew River would be fine, River would never be a target.

Zellendine, on the other hand, he just tightened his hold on her.

"The smell is amazing," she muttered, her smile a fixed

feature on her face as her feet picked carefully along the uneven and changing surface of the ground.

"Can you see the spindle yet?" he asked, no one and anyone, just hoping it was already cutting through the atmosphere and about to land.

But he didn't see anything, and no one answered him.

"When do I see the yawx and walk through the trees?" she asked, leaning out and looking around him to the tree line.

"Not today."

Her grip on his back loosened a fraction and he looked harder for the damn spindle.

"It needs to get here."

"What?" she asked, standing up straight and looking up at him, her eyes widened, her mouth dropped open, and her other hand grasped the front of his uniform as she ducked even further under his arm.

Looking up into the sky, the pink swirled as it changed into purple at its center.

"Everybody, heads up," Corto yelled, also spotting it.

The purple flew towards them, not in the too fast to follow speed it often traveled at, and not quite as relaxed as it had before.

"Zellendine, if I say duck, you do it, okay?" His voice low and steady, the hand he didn't have wrapped around her raised and ready.

"Troylus, I think I see the spindle too," Imogene said, pointing into the sky.

And yes, the spindle stabbed through the clouds and headed toward the clearing right in front of them.

He took a deep breath and blew it out, too much was happening at once, but he clenched his jaw and straightened his back.

While the spindle neared, the purple circled, like it was keeping an eye on the landing.

"Shit," he yelled, and eyes glanced toward him before they went back to watching the spindle and the threat.

"Is there something *else* to worry about?" Imogene yelled, River waking up and squirming so she put him to her shoulder and patted his back.

"Do we have a list of who is on the spindle?"

"Yeah, but I only remember a few of the names, why?" Corto said.

"What are the chances one of them is like Zellendine and Mason?"

Eyes, all their eyes turned toward him and her place, under his arm.

"Fuck," Zellendine muttered. "Okay, we need to get to the door of the spindle before they even open it, warn them to get back from it and have Rullon or Indigo open it up. They'll be most likely to be okay without testing, or anyone with silver eyes."

Troylus froze, not sure if he should turn around and run Zellendine back to safety, if it would alert the purple, or if he should try and shove her into the landing spindle the first chance he got.

"We need to get River and Zellendine back inside, and move everyone else one at a time." He knew the best way to do that was to wait until the spindle landed and coordinate with the people inside, but his feet itched to run Zellendine back.

"Is that the Wheel?" Corto asked, pointing just past where the purple circled.

"Yeah, but why is there light coming from it?" Imogene asked.

And there was, a beam of light piercing through a spot on the edge of the Wheel that they could make out through the gentle light of the morning. It must have been so bright in space it could rival the sun.

Zellendine ripped herself from his side and sprinted back to the door.

"No, what are you doing?" he yelled, darting after her.

"It's going to blow, like before, I have to send the message," she screamed.

Her voice was like a trigger; the purple went from its patterned surveillance to hurtling toward them.

She ran harder, not even looking up at the thing stalking her.

But she wasn't going to make it.

There was no way she was going to get to the drop panel in time, let alone get it lowered and be down the tunnel far enough for it not to hit her.

With his hands out in front of him, he screamed and threw his blue light at Zellendine with everything he had, wishing for her to be safe in the tunnels.

A tree and dirt swirled around her and swallowed her.

The only thing left by the time the purple stopped in place, was what looked like an over large stump.

He held his breath, keeping his hands ready, until it turned and left.

"Zellendine," he yelled, skidding to a stop in front of the stump and desperately patting at it.

"I'm fine, this goes down to a tunnel. I'll send the message. Go get everyone." Her voice trailed off at the end of her last sentence, like she was already moving.

He bent over and braced himself on his knees for a second before he turned back and ran for the clearing, where the spindle was driving the tip into the ground on landing.

Corto and the others stood back a step, while Imogene neared the landing area.

"Too close," he yelled, waving his hands over his head.

She had River and she was so close the spindle could upset the ground enough to send her flying.

"What are you doing?"

No one could hear him over the sound of a deafening roar.

The sound buffeted him, he threw his arm over his face and looked up into the sky.

Beyond the edge of the atmosphere, way out in space, the Wheel shattered in a storm of flames.

A strange dusting of sparkling ash seemed to fall among the clouds and sunbeams.

In the sky, the purple faded to nothing, and even the pink streaks wafted away as if blown by a stiff wind.

51

ZELLENDINE

"Are you sure this is going to work?" Xander asked, standing back with his arms crossed and his brow furrowed.

"Yes." She had never questioned it.

"But, how does it work?" he asked.

"That," she said, smiling at the prototype mechanical womb, "even I can't explain. I told Mohammed and the others all the information I knew about the process in the human body, and they worked together to build this."

"Well," Mohammed said over his shoulder, "we had a little help."

She turned to look at Troylus as he carried bags full of their supplies toward the main hallway.

"Hopefully it works," Imogene said, appearing next to her with Rullon who had River in his arms and was making funny faces at him. "And we can figure out how to get to word to other regions that they can do the same."

"If you do, let me know if they have any questions," Zellendine said, with a smile for the baby who laughed at his grandfather.

"And how will we do that?" Rullon asked, his voice the sing song he always addressed the baby with, but the words just for her. "There are no comms, and you're going too far away."

"We will be back a lot. I promise." She leaned over and kissed his cheek, but she didn't take the baby. Not yet.

They still had the rest of the day and that night to say good-bye. But their place was up the mountain, deep in the woods.

And it was ready.

It had only taken Troylus a month to get there, do the work, and get back.

Now, she was going to see it too, and they would make it as much of a home as the spindle, buried in the ground, had become.

Thank you for reading!

If you enjoyed this book please leave a review at your favorite vendor.

If you would like to be the first to know about the other books by the author, including the next book in this world, and get a free ebook in The Grimm Star Universe, head on over to

jdarleneeverly.com and sign up for the newsletter.

This is the last book in The Grimm Star Saga: First Light trilogy, but there are more stories coming in this world and many others.

ACKNOWLEDGMENTS

A whole hearted thank you to Bean, the Rottens, and all of my friends and family. A big bag of thanks to Jupiter Alley and Beth with Magnolia editing for their help in making this happen, as well as the team at Wishing Well. Sometimes, determination and strength are super powers.